C000049565

THE *Life* AND *Times* *Peeps McAvoy*

Growing Up and Old in the Hood

J. MICHAEL JEFFERS

© J. Michael Jeffers 2021

ISBN: 978-1-66781-753-8

eBook ISBN: 978-1-66781-754-5

All rights reserved. This book or any portion thereof may not be reproduced or used in any manner whatsoever without the express written permission of the publisher except for the use of brief quotations in a book review.

For the dreamers of dreams

CHAPTER ONE:
The Bus

What a wonderful urban experience Chicago is. It boasts a thriving city center where hundreds of thousands live and work. Its architecture was, and is, historically significant and one of the most cutting edge in the world. The city shines with thousands of acres of parks, plazas and beaches for riding, walking and swimming. The city was built on hundreds of sturdy and stable neighborhoods which ring the Loop. Chicago's transit system is clean, modern and efficient. Well mostly. This CTA bus began at the trashy turn-around at Arthur and Clark, chugged like an ancient behemoth east on Devon and became the Broadway bus number 36, going south all the way to the Loop and beyond to the Des Plaines and Harrison Terminal. Something unusual about Broadway is that it has no avenue, street, road or court after its name; but there is one street sign that labels it as Broadway Avenue—obviously the work of an overzealous sign worker at Streets and Sanitation. In total there were 76 official stops en route. This bus was famous for three reasons: the monster belched diesel exhaust as it travelled through some of the most expensive real estate in the city (making it a stinking mess inside and out); the heating and air conditioning on most vehicles rarely worked (roasting riders in summer and freezing them in winter); and despite what the CTA said, it stopped more than 76 times (the slowest land transportation in city history). Despite its limitations, it had its fans.

Peeps McAvoy was among them. At 55 years of age he had been retired for two years and loved the fact that all sorts of people rode the bus. Mostly young and old, all different races; some skinny, but most on the larger size of life. Burdened with packages and parcels from the Post Office, shopping bags, purses and children, they climbed on and off as real veterans of old Number 36. Peeps found it amazing the amount of crap that could be crammed into the bus, especially around Dominick's Finer Foods and the Target store in Uptown. Number 36 was the segue to some serious shopping for the average folks who lived in senior citizen apartments on, or near, Broadway. Where the other people came from was a complete mystery as Edgewater and Uptown had long been gentrified and were increasingly white and very middle class. No bus riders in that crowd.

Bus time, like prison time, is a long time; while traveling, Peeps needed a diversion. One of Peeps' favorite mental gymnastics was to make up stories about people who came on and off Number 36. He gave people made-up names. He speculated on where they lived and with whom. He studied them thoroughly, but carefully so as not to appear strange. Having said that, what exactly was normal on Number 36? The bar was pretty low as far as Peeps could see. The longer the victim rode, the more time Peeps had to assemble a mental persona. A good looking woman naturally allowed him the opportunity to dissect her sex life; what her partner, he or she, might look like; how often did they have sex and where? Is she cheating on someone? If so, how long has the affair lasted? If he worked this long enough he might have her undressed in his mind, even to the point of being mildly aroused. He had the entire return trip on the bus to fill in the details and to enhance his sketch, to the point when he settled at the tavern in the late afternoon, usually the Double Bubble, he would begin his fable de jour for his drinking mates. Naturally, it took several pints of Guinness and mild prompting to get him started. The lads were often disappointed if Peeps failed to come up with a fine yarn. Talking about the same old bullshit night after night was boring—last place Cubs, latest Alderman to be indicted or the state or cost of everything. Peeps could tell a fine tale, and he got better at his craft as the beverages added up and years went on.

Anyone who first met Peeps was mildly perplexed by his name. Born Andrew Thomas McAvoy in the year of our Lord 1960, the last of four children of the McAvoys on Hood Street (as opposed to the Glenwood Avenue mob of nine kids), he came by his nickname honestly. The story was this: At age four Peeps loved Easter, especially the marshmallow candies in the form of chicks and rabbits. At four o'clock on Easter morning he got up to get an early start on his Easter basket. But why stop there, Peeps reasoned. The Sisters and The Brother also had baskets with a goodly supply of his favorites. And they were still in bed. All's fair in love and Easter baskets. Climbing back into bed, he was sated and very proud of himself. Not a marshmallow critter left in the house.

Easter breakfast was a real feast. While the Old Man slept off the four to eleven police shift and substantial bourbon and beer, the rest of the family settled down to pancakes, fresh orange juice, bacon and sausages. What a treat, as the usual fare was cold cereal. Nanna even lit candles and said grace before anyone could attack the food. Suddenly, a horrible gurgling noise came from Andy; he got violently ill, puking over the entire table. The other children fled in horror with poor Nanna faced with the consequences. Cleanup was punctuated with much yelling, swearing and hair pulling, especially when The Sisters and The Brother discovered that their baskets had been raided. Not a single marshmallow candy in sight.

Once this disaster was taken care of, it was time to get washed a second time before setting off for Mass at St. Gertrude's Catholic Church. Andrew had been crying from the moment he left home and continued to snivel throughout Mass. He was relegated to the end of the pew near the aisle, the pariah that he was. A private spectacle was one thing, but a public one was another matter entirely. And sure enough, the Pariah came through in spades. Vomiting violently during the Gospel while everyone was standing—and a good thing too—people from three pews away fled the debacle. No one knew what to do. The priest simply went on with his reading and the sermon as though nothing had happened. The ushers were not going to clean it up; they were all in suits and ties. Nanna did the only thing she could; she grabbed Andy by the shirt collar and fled, stopping at the bathroom in the vestibule to clean the little bugger up.

Andy was relegated to his bed for the day and Nanna thought it was as good a time as ever to bring out the Jameson. Never shy herself, she had two shots and promptly fell asleep on the couch, where The Sisters and The Brother found her softly snoozing. By the time of the next Mass, everyone in the neighborhood knew the story. It was a month before Nanna went back to Sunday Mass and she took a pew on the other side of the church, as far away as possible from the scene of the crime. The most horrified was the Burnham family—lace curtain Irish who were sure they were better than anyone else. Many at church that day secretly thought it very funny that the Burnhams had to leave in total humiliation, as they were sitting in the pew in front of the McAvoys. Of course there was spillage on Mrs. Burnham. She had left for church fifteen minutes early decked out in a white chiffon dress with a light green jacket, with shoes to match, naturally. The showstopper was a white straw hat with a green ribbon that went down her back. Mrs. B was not beautiful, but she caught everyone's attention that morning with the huge oversized bonnet. The hat took the worst of it.

No one had ever seen a parishioner get up in the middle of the homily and yell *shit* as loudly as she did that morning; the church was as silent as a mausoleum as everyone, including the priest, stared in astonishment. Father thought his homily was not that great, but certainly did not deserve such public ridicule. How could she face her neighbors and friends after this debacle? Everyone, absolutely everyone, would be talking about her for months; and she was right.

The Burnhams had a reputation of a family on the way up. St. Gertrude School was not good enough for their three kids. They attended the Academy of the Sacred Heart on Sheridan Road, where many of Chicago's swells sent their children. Considered the *creme de la creme* of parochial schools, it attracted families up and down the Outer Drive, Michigan Avenue and the Gold Coast. While successful by most standards, Mr. Burnham was merely a high level bureaucrat in the City's Department of Transportation. Many a wag in the neighborhood thought they were living well beyond their means. They sure acted and talked like they were set for life, but there were obvious signs of fraying on their lace curtains. While Nanna never cared for the bossy Mrs.

Burnham, never in her wildest dreams did she feel they deserved to be soiled at Mass by her four year old.

Andrew was no more; with unfailing neighborhood brutality he was now and forever rechristened Peeps. Even the Sisters at school called him by his nickname. He was traumatized at four years of age. Despite it all, he never refused a marshmallow chick or rabbit; he still loved them. They were his favorite.

Peeps liked to wait for No. 36 in front of the Chicago Public Library, Edgewater branch. There were benches and they were a great relief to his aching left foot and ankle, hurt years ago from an accident at work. The bus was so damn slow. The schedule was non-existent. Naturally, one bus pulled up while another was a block away. The first packed to the gills, the second almost empty. Of course, this was long before the fancy apps you downloaded on your phone that timed a bus to the minute. Because he was in no hurry, Peeps always waited for a bus with seating available. Standing was a torture, even for the healthiest rider. Stopping, starting, lurching forward at a snail's pace, standing riders were exhausted after a mile.

His goal most days was the Newberry Library in the Gold Coast. Huron and State was stop number 51, and just a few blocks from the library steps. And he was a man on a mission. Peeps was fascinated by the library. The Newberry was one of those great institutions that grew out of a growing appetite for learning, research and scholarly inquiry in the humanities. Open to the public for free since its founding in 1887, it was the product of the benevolence of Walter Loomis Newberry and was graced by the surrounding leafy Washington Square. The library did not lend books and materials, but rather made its collection available to patrons on site only. Peeps was fascinated with history, and history was what the Newberry was all about. He particularly liked the history of Chicago and its tremendous growth during and after the Civil War. Visiting two, sometimes three days a week, Peeps became a fixture at the history desk and very comfortable with the head research librarian, Vivian. An amiable Black woman of inestimable age, she had progressed over the years to head of the department from the lowly position restocking books, courtesy of a University of Chicago master's degree in library science and an advanced degree in American history.

Ms. Vivian was both impressed by Peeps and often annoyed. Peeps came prepared with his yellow pads of copious notes from previous visits. He took up an entire table, noisily crumpled paper, sighed loudly and generally asked two dozen questions in a single morning. Most annoying, he never came with a pencil or pen. Somehow, he thought it was Vivian's responsibility to supply them. Vivian finally gave up and had a coffee mug labeled "Peeps' pencils" and stored them at a convenient arm's reach. She increasingly and begrudgingly admired Peep, his interest in history, and the fact that he had only a few hours of undergraduate work under his belt. She admired his intellectual curiosity and his commitment to his hobby. Rather than sitting around watching *The Price Is Right*, he took the initiative to read, study, and improve himself. But he was an odd character and often a royal pain in the ass.

Peeps was very curious about Ms. Vivian. She was at least ten years older and very much in control of her department. They were strangers who made time at the library to work and shared information and ideas. But Peeps was a "nosy parker," as the old phrase goes. What made her tick? Was she married? He thought not as she had no ring and was rather plain in her makeup and clothing style. He did learn that she had a condo in Hyde Park, the bastion of the lake-front liberals and the world famous University of Chicago. By assumption, he felt that she was liberal in her politics and enjoyed the rarified university world of which she was a part. Another staff member had told Peeps, in a moment of indiscretion, that she owned a very nice, 1940s co-op with her elderly mother. Lakefront property in Hyde Park was prohibitively expensive, especially in the tony, older buildings that formed a concrete hedge along the Outer Drive. A librarian's salary, even at the world-famous Newberry, could not cover the fees and other amenities of co-op living. This same staffer hinted at family money, but not from life insurance or a legacy. Further scientific inquiry, simply paying attention to her name badge, told Peeps what he really needed to know. Her surname was Jackson and with some searching he found out that Vivian was the only daughter of a long-time politico from the Southeast side who was known to be as corrupt as Boss Tweed, the famous New York gangster-politician.

Alderman Jackson grew up in the 1940s in what was then the changing neighborhood of Englewood, many years later to be the home of some of the most violent crimes in the history of Chicago. As was often the case, he was raised by a single mother who hustled at a local diner by day and babysat in the evenings to make ends meet. In time, she qualified for food stamps and subsidized housing. One thing that Ms. Jackson did not do was get pregnant again. She saw what happened to other girls, having baby after baby with no education, resources or opportunity. She had lovers, quite a few over the years, but insisted on condoms. She had a hard enough time managing Walter and the streets; she could not imagine taking care of a brood.

It turns out Walter, or W, as he was called, was both bright and precocious. He could do very well in school if he felt like it. Often his school success depended on whether he liked his teacher or not. At times, he felt that he was smarter than they were. He sensed that many of them resented teaching in an increasingly Black neighborhood. Some were downright smug and condescending; others outright racist. When not in school, he was supposed to go home and report to the neighbor lady that he was, in fact, home. Once reporting, he simply went out the back door to hang out with his friends. His crimes were small, as he knew his mother would kick his ass if he got into real trouble: smoking, stealing from the local stores and generally being obnoxious, particularly around the neighborhood girls.

High school was a different matter. W hung around with a mixed bunch. Two friends were really good in school; the others skipped class as much as they attended. Tyrell and William were solid working class kids, with fathers who worked in the Ford assembly plant in South Chicago. They made a decent living and kept proper households. It was William's father who caught W alone one day and asked flat out if he were a stupid shit. Taken aback, and before he could respond, he got a good old-fashioned tongue lashing about what a hapless, lazy boy he was—especially because he had brains and talent and a mother who cared a great deal.

Stung by the humiliation, he went home as angry as he had ever been in his life. The resentment raged for days. He refused to leave his room, not for school and not even to hang around with friends. He skipped meals and talked back to his mother, something he never did. Finally, after a week of this, Ms. Jackson had enough. She marched into his room and demanded to be told what was going on. After nearly an hour of sulking and silence he retold the story of William's father and his total condemnation of W and the way he was living his life. Nothing was resolved until the next night when Ms. Jackson went to pick up W's report card. He had failed history and geometry, not having bothered to take the mid-term exams.

The shit hit the fan, and big time. W and Ms. Jackson engaged in a forty-minute staring contest, with her holding the grade sheet and giving him the evil eye as never before. W had two choices she told him: go to school, hang with the right kids and get good grades or drop out of school in two months when he was sixteen and get a job. W could not believe what the old lady was saying to him: get a job! For the first time in his life, he was truly afraid. He was a kid. He could not imagine doing something like his mother was doing—working for minimum wage. Even he knew that if he dropped out the only jobs available were dull and low paying. He thought about getting involved with a gang, but that idea scared the shit out of him too. He did not have the balls to sell drugs, steal and shoot people. The gangs were all around and he knew what they were about. He guessed that he would be dead in five years if he went that route.

W decided to seek the advice of the only two people he could talk to: Tyrell and William. After a particularly nasty day at school—confrontations with both history and geometry teachers—he met his buddies at his house and confessed what had been happening and his mother's ultimatum. His brothers came through; they offered to help get him back on track in school and they planned study sessions every week. Everyone knew it would take little time for W to get back in stride. By the time he was a senior his grades were good enough, so he applied to, and was admitted with a full scholarship to DePaul University (the other Catholic university in town). He finished in three and one-half years with a respectable B average.

During university time, he managed to find part-time work at the local Democratic precinct office. He began to learn how the system worked. He made friends with merchants and political types in the area. In the course of two years he became a serious young man with ambitions. One of his first deals was to get his mother into a new subsidized housing complex in the South Shore neighborhood—a once very white bastion on the South Side. Friends, even the alderman, suggested that he go to law school. He applied to DePaul and just made it in. The school knew him and took a chance even though his LSAT scores were low by university standards.

School was exhausting and he often fell behind. He joined study groups and managed with some grit to end school with a C+ average. The Illinois State Bar Exam was another matter entirely. He took it four times and finally passed on the fourth try. He hung out his shingle in Hyde Park and specialized in nothing. He would represent anyone with cash. He had a part-time assistant who knew as much law as he did. The legal practice was a means to an end. He wanted in on the easy money that came through politics on the precinct level. He wanted to be an alderman in the worst way. He lost his first attempt in the South Shore neighborhood. But luck was with him. The standing alderman was indicted four months after being re-elected and W used every contact he had to get the mayor's attention. It was just a matter of time before the current alderman would resign. The Feds had him on tape soliciting and taking bribes on seventeen different occasions. W assured the mayor's cronies that he was their man. Over twenty years he kept his word and voted with the mayor and the machine at every single roll call. He was a good and faithful servant (albeit an increasingly rich and corrupt one). He hustled, too, keeping tabs on everything going on in his ward. He helped people with problems: landlords, permit applications, an empty lot that needed cleaning out. You name it and he did it for his neighbors. All for a fee of course. He wanted to be an alderman for many years to come.

As the South Shore neighborhood continued to go from white to black, there was almost no economic development or residential building. W could make money helping existing businesses and landlords—for a fee of course—but this had limited potential. Eventually Alderman W found the pot of gold: fixing traffic tickets. How he did it, no one ever figured out. Twenty dollars was the standard fee, which was not unreasonable considering that the city increased traffic fines almost every year. W never charged more than twenty bucks. On Saturdays and Sundays the line to his office was down the street. Everyone knew what was going on, but how he got away with it was a total mystery. W was very careful to never accept money directly, but rather asked petitioners to make a twenty dollar contribution to his charitable fund. He never discussed business over the phone and had no written records that anyone ever found. If the business at hand had great potential, the deal was discussed on a walk along the lakefront, or during a high school basketball game or at a local greasy spoon. We did not look good in an orange jumpsuit and he had no intention of going to jail.

W never discussed his business with friends or colleagues; neither his wife nor his daughter had any idea what was going on (or they chose not to know). His real wealth came from his real estate holdings, which were always on the safe—and white—north side. Slowly, he amassed a portfolio of thirty apartment buildings and a dozen or so commercial properties, and all with stable tenants. By his tenth year in office, W got out of the ticket fixing business and put his full attention to his growing real estate empire.

It was pretty obvious that Walter wanted to protect his only child from the slings and arrows of Chicago politics. His daughter would never have to take a bribe or fix a building permit.

Very interesting person, this Ms. Vivian, thought Peeps. He would need to learn more about what made her tick. He would invite her to a local coffee shop and get the ball rolling. One day. He was a nosy bastard.

Once in a while, a visit to the library included lunch at Bob's Burgers, one of the many new, hip burger joints that populated the Gold Coast. A few blocks from the library—and late enough to avoid the noon rush—Peeps used this meal as both lunch and dinner most days. While not preoccupied with health, he was savvy enough to know that a diet of slop burgers three times a week would probably kill him. And due to the damage to his ankle, any extensive exercise was out of the question. Although he could well afford it, twenty dollars a pop was expensive, but a bacon and cheddar two hours before martinis at the Double Bubble seemed a proper way for a near gentleman to spend his days.

At just over six feet, Peeps was still reasonably good looking. He handled himself with a bit more care than most of the slobs at the tavern. He was careful about his hygiene and his hair. He shaved every other day—needed or not—and he visited Father and Son's barber shop on Broadway about every six weeks. The barber shop was an amazing place: no matter how many barbers they hired—there were seven now—the place was always packed. The wait was often more than an hour and seating was hard to find. As a regular, the owners knew that Peeps could not stand long and always managed to find an extra chair from the closet for him, even as others stood. A few dirty looks could easily be ignored. When he limped to the barber chair, everyone in attendance would understand. And if they didn't, who gave a shit.

The barber shop was a cash machine. Debit or credit cards were not accepted. Most of the habitues were much younger than Peeps. Two-thirds of them had serious beards, which was all the fashion. Trimming hair and a beard took considerable time. And accounted for a long wait. In short order, the twelve dollar haircut became twenty (plus tip of course). But what puzzled Peeps the most was the number of men around during the day, seemingly without employment, or more likely working for themselves or as freelancers. His other complaint was that the noise in the place was deafening. The customers mostly sat brooding on their smartphones and made little conversation. The noise was from the barbers. Everyone talked more than they cut. And they were loud and profane. Even the lady barber could keep up with her mates. While Peeps always got a quality haircut, on most occasions he could not wait to get the hell out.

Like most neighborhoods, the focal point—other than the church—were the taverns. For Peeps' liking, he found four to be very convenient and serviceable. All were within four blocks of each other: the Sovereign, the Pumping Company, Double Bubble, and The Cellars.

The first, the Sovereign, opened early—eight o'clock to be exact and closed at two a.m. —the drinkers were all over sixty, and most were retired and with serious problems (drinking or otherwise). They came early and often to get out of the house and away from their wives. But the joint had a real split personality. The evening traffic, after work, brought groups of gay men. Diverse clientele aside, the Sovereign was a bare bones establishment. Nothing fancy on the menu; there was no menu. Shots, beer, and a few mixed drinks were the order of the day. The food was limited to the snack rack of weeks old potato chips and pretzels, but the limitations did not seem to hurt business.

The Pumping Company was a premier establishment; it served as much food as it did booze. The menu was typical of a tavern: burgers, tacos, salads and similar items. The food was good and inexpensive. At least once a week, Peeps showed up for martinis, conversation, and dinner. Of the four, there were more women in this bar than the others. The place was packed by neighborhood regulars on Friday and Saturday evenings. The greetings were friendly, the conversation affable, and the wait long. As a result, Peeps avoided the weekends because there was no place to sit waiting for a table.

The Cellars was a warm, cheery place where everyone knew your name. It was a restaurant, however, not a bar, and though they served cold martinis and had a serviceable wine list, Peeps was particularly fond of their New Year's Eve sittings (three in all, depending on your sleep tolerance). The younger crowd usually ate dinner late, at the third setting, thus ready for twelve o'clock. The Cellars was the perfect place for a second or third date. Peeps loved the joint.

But of the four, the Bubble was Peeps' preferred establishment. Saints and sinners, businessmen and bums would stop in for a favored beverage and a good argument. The place was always lively, even in the middle of the day. Working guys would stop for a beer and a burger, to be replaced by customers from the neighborhood for an after-work drink. The bar keep, knowing that Peeps would typically show up most evenings, put a bottle of Tanqueray gin and a martini glass in the ice so that both were very cold. He also made a point of stocking extra-large green olives as garnish. Peeps was a valued customer.

This friendly place was schizophrenic though; on Friday and Saturday nights, it would often turn rowdy. Larry, the owner, had a hell of a time controlling the arguments that turned into fights. They were uncanny in their regularity. There was pushing and shoving naturally, but real fist fights would start, either in the bar or out on Broadway. There were always off-duty cops around, so the police were never called. What caused ordinarily pleasant neighbors to turn ugly to the point of a bar room brawl was hard to understand. Peeps made it a point to leave before seven on Fridays and never came in on Saturdays.

After cocktails and boring his friends with long tales, Peeps tottered home, north on Broadway and west on Hood. By the time he got home, he was exhausted. It had been a long, hot July day and he just wanted to sit and listen to the quiet. Once the air conditioning was humming, Peeps fixed a light gin and tonic, grabbed the *Tribune* and headed to the front porch. There was still plenty of light to read and certainly time to relax. He still missed Nanna. She would always chat, if she were up, after work or whenever he came home. He missed her company. After all, he was a mama's boy through and through.

With a loud sigh, he laughed about the day. His nosey detection worked on Ms. Vivian and especially the fat lady on the bus. When he told this story at the Bubble, no one believed him. They thought it was one of his long tales. But it was not. As Number 36 got to the Wilson Avenue stop, there was a fairly long line of people waiting to get on, many from the junior college across the street. At the head of the line was the fattest lady he had ever seen. She was enormous, surely four hundred pounds or more, a veritable block of sweating humanity.

The task at hand was to get her on the bus. She did not fit through the double doors going straight in. She had to turn sideways. She got to the first step and got stuck. Fortunately, her companion—one fifth her size—was there to help. She took a running start and plowed into her hip to move her further.

Four attempts later and the lady was still not on the bus. The driver put the bus in neutral and did his best to pull her in; between pushing and pulling, a full five or six minutes passed. Finally, to the cheers of the very impatient riders, she made it in and on, and flopped on the first available seat (the one kept clear for handicapped riders). Peeps wondered almost aloud how she would get out. Ah, city living: one certainly would not see this happening in a prim and proper suburban setting such as Barrington.

After saying good night to a few neighbors out walking dogs, Peeps watched the news and the hapless Cubs who were playing a night game in Los Angeles. Cub watching was the perfect antidote to insomnia. By the time the ten o'clock news finished, the Cubs were behind by five runs. Would they ever win a pennant? He fell sound asleep on the couch and dreamt of becoming a White Sox fan.

CHAPTER TWO:
Nanna

Helen Anne Flynn was born in February of 1928. She was the first born of John and Audrey of St. Timothy Parish in the West Rogers Park neighborhood. Like those around them, they were working class Irish and Germans—many working in City government as cops, firemen, garbage collectors and in white-collar jobs at City Hall. John and Audrey eventually had three daughters and managed to keep a roof over their heads throughout the Great Depression—but only barely. As the thirties ground on, John often worked only three or four days and did not get a raise for eight years. His security job at city council was secure if uneven (technically, he was a policeman and not a security guard). Audrey did her best to find small jobs babysitting, caring for an aging upstairs neighbor or whatever she could find. Their commitment to a Catholic education for their children made their finances more strained. Two dollars per child a month in 1945 was a fortune.

Helen, her mother, grandparents and everyone else they knew hated her name and referred to her as Annie. Her father, John, loved it because the name came from one of his obscure cousins still living in County Clare, just south of Galway Bay, Ireland. The American Flynns had absolutely no contact with the cousins and no one could figure John's passion for the name Helen. For the rest of her life, he was the only person to call her by her birth name. At some point in time, even before becoming a grandmother, Annie became Nanna. Sometimes, matters evolve without rhyme or reason.

By the middle of the 1940s, John's work was stable and he was even promoted to supervisor for daytime security. But the world was also a very frightening place. The American government was increasingly alarmed by the Germans and Japanese, and began drafting men in ever larger numbers. Preference was given to unmarried, younger men. Due to his age—and the fact that he had three girls—he managed to escape the draft deluge, but there was always the possibility of him being taken if actual war broke out.

Annie graduated from St. Tim's and was destined for St. Scholastica Academy on Ridge Boulevard in east Rogers Park. The school was well staffed with Benedictine sisters, so the tuition was reasonable, but fifteen dollars a month—with two more Flynn girls to follow—was still a tremendous burden. Belts were tightened, the old beater kept running and occasional assistance from the grandparents helped balance the budget. There was no other option. St. Scholastica was the best girls' school on the north side. Girls came from the suburbs of Evanston, Wilmette and Lincolnwood because of the quality education that students received. The school had a great atmosphere, dedicated staff, advanced classes in math and science and was superb preparation for college or a career. The sisters ran a tight ship, but were loving and committed. Annie loved high school and was consistently in the top half of her class.

Peeps rarely heard stories about his mother's upbringing. There were photos of course and his aunts would tell tales—apparently Nanna was quite the feisty one. She loved to test the sisters' patience and rules, and occasionally found herself in detention. She particularly liked every boy she ever met and was willing to flirt at the drop of a hat. The boys from St. George and Loyola Academy were all around. She went to every sock hop either school held. With her gang of friends, she met the boys at the beach in the summer and for skating parties in the winter. Her parents enjoyed the young people and did not mind having them around. The Flynn family often hosted small parties—better to have the boys and girls close by rather than off somewhere unsupervised, they thought.

Annie enjoyed the traditional classes the best: History, English, and particularly Art. She spent as much free time as possible—outside of babysitting—to practice sketching; she used all of her free money for art supplies. While her work was not exceptional, it was good enough to get the sisters' attention. She competed both in school and at regional art fairs (often coming home with blue second place ribbons).

While Annie was not the prettiest or most popular in school, the phone rang early and often at the Flynn household when the weekends approached. Junior and senior years were a whirl of dances, football games, homework and babysitting. With close counsel from her mother and the indirect influence of the sisters at school, Annie knew what *not* to do. She would remain a good Catholic girl until marriage, no matter how much the boys begged and pleaded. God forbid she would ever have to explain a pregnancy at seventeen years of age to her parents. The entire family would be humiliated. How different the standard would be twenty-five years later, but this was then and the rules were the rules. With sharp elbows and a good squirm, Annie got out of lots of close calls.

After graduation, Annie found an entry-level customer service job at Bell & Howell, the well-respected camera maker that was a veritable Chicago institution. The home office and factory were in Lincolnwood (with a Chicago address). The week before she started, she was in a panic. She needed clothes for work. With her mother's help, and the old Singer plugged in and ready to go, she had the entire house in an uproar with patterns and fabric everywhere. She had paid attention—back when she was interviewing—to what the other women wore to work. With her meager savings and twenty-five dollars from her father, she took the El down to the Carson's store on State Street to purchase what she could not make.

Annie did not own a car, so commuting to work took time and some creativity. She had a six block walk from the bus stop to the office—not bad in the summer, but a real horror during Chicago's long winters. Her first major purchase was a substantial winter coat. And since she was still living at home, she gave her parents fifty dollars a month for room and board. The rest was hers and she saved most of it. After six months on the job she felt rich. Her goal was to buy a car—nothing special—just something that could safely get her to work and back.

Her social life was boring and she knew it. Most Friday nights she was too exhausted to even think about going out. She would take a quick bath, dress in pajamas and read or listen to the radio with her sisters and parents. Both sisters were now in high school, so Annie spent a lot of time listening, laughing, talking about the teachers, and of course, boys. When her sisters had plans—a date or some other activity—Annie stayed up to read the latest thriller she got from the library. Saturday nights, however, were spent with her girlfriends, or on an occasional date. She did not have anyone that she was serious about—she was only twenty—but one day she would meet someone she would want to marry.

On Saturday nights, her group usually headed for a rather nice bar on Lincoln Avenue called Lucky's. Even though she was not yet twenty-one, she could be served thanks to a very strange Illinois law that allowed women to be served at eighteen while men had to be twenty-one. For reasons no one could figure out, the law managed to stay in effect for almost ten years. Eventually, all drinkers had to be twenty-one. The end result was that the guys at Lucky's were a couple of years older than Annie and her friends. They were also a bit more mature and they even had manners (mostly).

After two years, Annie was promoted to assistant manager for the customer service department and was given her own office. The room was a shoebox with no window; hot as hell in the summer and freezing in the winter. But it was hers. She even had a door that closed. And more importantly, she got a raise of fifteen dollars a week—the money she needed to buy her first car. Right away, Annie found an elderly neighbor up the block that wanted to sell her old boat of a motor vehicle to move closer to her children in the suburbs. Annie and her father visited the neighbor, learned about the history of the car—how often the oil was changed and tires rotated—and, after being satisfied by the price of four hundred dollars, the two of them took it for a ride. Shortly thereafter, her father looked under the hood—as though he knew what he was looking at—

and Annie purchased her first car (a nineteen forty-six Chevy). It was perfect. And now she could ride to Lucky's in style.

Several months later, Annie was called into her manager's office. She panicked. She racked her brains to figure out what she had done wrong. As it turns out, her supervisor had a proposition for her: would she be willing to model the company's latest professional reflex camera? The ad would appear in trade publications and in company catalogs. She would be paid twenty-five dollars and the company would hold all rights to the images. She agreed on the spot and went to the sales department to sign a contract and plan the shooting. The next day, she was asked to bring her best winter coat; the shooting was taking place outside. Fortunately for Annie, her winter coat was the best item of clothing she owned. The shooting took the entire day (nearly thirty poses in all and from all sorts of angles). With a hat on her head and the large winter coat, Annie hardly recognized herself in the ad, and her friends did not believe her, so she had to bring the signed contract as proof. She did three more sittings in the next twelve months. It was glamorous. And Annie certainly was not glamorous. She could never figure out why she was chosen, and just as quickly as it began—shortly after her fourth shoot—her career as a model ended.

On a beautiful fall Saturday evening, the doors to Lucky's were wide open to let in the cool breeze. The place was packed; Annie and her friends had managed to squeeze into a corner of the bar toward the back where the servers worked their magic, remembering who ordered what and who had or had not paid. The system was a complete mystery to Annie as many regulars ran a tab which the bartender kept by the cash register. The girls were chatting and flirting with a group of guys that were a few years older. The tall one, very Irish with black hair and blue eyes, seemed quite interested in Annie. HIs name was Brian McAvoy and he was studying to take the exam to be a Chicago policeman. Annie was flattered and before leaving gave him her phone number. She was fairly certain that he would not call. But he did.

Despite some minor inconveniences—like his lack of a car—Brian and Annie managed to become a number. Quickly too. They often met at Lucky's when they got together, an occurrence which caused its own set of inconveniences. Brian seemed incapable of having a proper date (just the two of them). When he showed up at the tavern he was always with his friends. So it was a group date—guys in one squad and girls in another. Some of the others made friends with Brian's crowd, so it was very much fun all the way around. Because Brian was trying to get into the police academy, he had to be very careful about what he did and what he said. He liked to drink and worked very hard to keep his drinking in check (both to impress Annie and to make sure he did not get a reputation as a problem at the academy). Some nights Annie drove him home and—like everyone else in the crowd—he lived with his parents. His own apartment was out of the question on a part-time pay packet. Shoot, even after graduation, he would not make much. Chicago police were notoriously poorly paid, which contributed to the outsized level of petty corruption. At times, however, the corruption was not petty at all. Yearly, groups of officers and their superiors would be charged with theft, bribery and even violence in pursuit of easy cash. The cycle was endless. The sad part was that the offenders often got away with it; rarely did cases go to court. Punishment might be a week to a month without pay. If a citizen complained, matters were usually swept under a large rug. There was a code of silence and every young officer learned that lesson early on.

What made matters worse for so-called reformers was that a huge portion of police candidates were Irish. First, second and third generation Irish filled the rank and file and constituted the majority of commanders and lieutenants. Even in other ethnic neighborhoods the Irish cop was a fixture. North side Irish worked on the South side and South side Irish worked the North. It did not matter. The code of silence was reinforced by ethnic pride. It was like a huge fraternity; no one ratted on a brother officer. Their off-duty behavior tended to be boyish as well. There was rarely a reprimand. Naturally, drinking was a big part of the problem. And it was not just the Irish. Being a policeman and hard drinking were hand and glove. There was no solution but to have a private conversation with chronic offenders. And a visit with the chaplain did little to stem the problem. Brian was aware of issues both political and alcohol related, but his only desire was to follow father and uncles into the Chicago Police Department.

But he needed help. Naturally, he went to see his local Alderman who seemed to have undue influence on who passed and failed the dreaded police exam. Of course, Brian came with gifts. Also, Brian was not that well educated; Annie sensed that his schooling ended even before the eighth grade. His reading and writing skills were especially poor. Annie quietly listened to his concerns about the exam and at the first chance offered to study with him. She helped him fill out the application and write a letter as to why he wanted to be a police officer. She read and reread the test preparation book as though she were taking the exam. She thought the material was pretty basic, but did her best not to let on. They worked through the book, underlining important content. Each session she quizzed Brian on what they had studied the night before. When he got bored or restless, she nudged him to keep him working. Read, explain, quiz and all over again. She was quietly demonic to get her man the job he wanted. One month after taking the exam, Brian got the great news that he had passed and was due to report to the police academy in a month. Strangely, the Alderman told Brian with a smile, that he had finished in the top half of the class. The Alderman took the credit, but Brian knew the real credit went to Annie.

The invitation to join the academy included a strongly worded message about alcohol and physical fitness. Cadets must pass a blood test given randomly and run a mile, do twenty push-ups, thirty sit-ups and other physical skills. Brian lost weight, got together with two guys he knew were going to the academy and worked out, and the three of them improved their physical endurance. Between work and working out, Brian did not have much time for Annie. But she was a prudent and patient young woman.

When they did go out and Annie drove Brian home, he took advantage to scoot over and sit close to her. He loved the smell of her hair and it afforded him a chance to try to cop a feel or two before they showed up at his apartment. Increasingly, the romancing got heavier as they stopped at the curb. But Annie was up to the task; with sharp elbows and lots of squirming she managed to get loose and send a very frustrated and very horny young man out of the car. He begged her to get into the back seat with him, but with charm and a smile, she always turned him down. As her mother, in so many words would say, no milk without buying the cow. Annie wanted marriage and stability—not one night stands in the back of a dirty Chevy.

The next time Brian called Annie she declined his offer to meet at Lucky's; she told him outright that she wanted a proper date (just the two of them). She would help pay and it could be as simple as pizza and beer. She was determined to know Brian, to find out what he was really like. Did he go to church? What were his interests other than drinking and gambling on the ponies. Did he have a plan for the future? Had he thought about going back to school? Did he read or like the movies? Annie wanted to know about his family and his friends. Brian got the hint and the next week—on Friday and Saturday—it was just Annie and Brian. First for pizza and then to the movies. They both had a great time and both were smitten. The next step was to bring Brian home to her parents. She did and her family absolutely loved him. He had started at the Academy, so he came dressed in his police formal uniform and that sealed the deal.

Within six months, Brian asked John Flynn for his daughter's hand in marriage. John had some reservations primarily because Brian was going to be a cop. John knew a cop's life (marriages often ending in separation or divorce). Over a beer, he told Brian in no certain terms that he expected that his daughter would be taken care of and that he, Brian, had a lot of growing up to do. Brian sweated like a leaky bucket and was grateful for the evening to end and even more pleased that John still approved of the marriage.

With a dozen roses handy, which he hid in the bushes by his house, Brian asked Annie to step out of the car. Annie was tired and just wanted to go home, but Brian persisted. He wanted to talk more. He retrieved the roses, and with the ring in his other hand, knelt down and asked her to be his wife. Suddenly, Annie was not tired anymore and she eagerly accepted his offer; she was crying and laughing at the same time and could hardly speak. She had never been happier. Brian placed his grandmother's engagement ring—a small diamond mounted on white gold—on her shaking hand. It took two attempts (Brian kept dropping the ring and laughing). While the diamond was not huge, it was a beautiful piece of jewelry, which fortunately fit perfectly (he did not have the money to get the bloody thing sized). Both thought that was a good omen of things to come. The kids decided to spend Sunday after mass, with Brian in attendance, at her house to make plans. Weddings were always on Saturday mornings if there was a full Mass with Communion and a brunch afterwards, and since most of the responsibility fell on the bride's parents, a wedding was a major hit to the wallet. The Flynns, unbeknown to Annie, had set aside her fifty dollars room and board from the outset to save for this very occasion.

Brian would be out of the academy by the end of the summer and would get a decent bump in raise, so they could afford a small apartment and a second beater for Brian. The wedding would take place at St. Tim's and they rented the party room next door to Lucky's for the reception. Gus, who owned both places, promised the room would be great. Brian could not get time off, so the couple planned a long three day weekend over Labor Day and found a cabin at Starved Rock State Park, about two hours outside of Chicago. Traditionally, the groom paid for the rehearsal dinner and booze at the reception. Brian had to hustle to cover his portion of the wedding costs. He found part-time work at Wrigley Field as a security guard and spent as much of the summer as he could working his part-time gig. He stayed away from betting and he was too busy to spend much on drinks at Lucky's. He lost more weight and saved money like mad.

The families met. Bridesmaids and groomsmen were chosen. Invitations were sent out in the mail. And a caterer was soon chosen. The whole affair worked like a well-oiled machine. Annie-with help from her mother—not only made her dress, but those for her three friends who were standing up. Every penny possible was saved, including limiting the number invited to the reception to about fifty guests. Because Brian was always working, Annie even had time to make two new dresses and casual shirts for the daytime for the honeymoon. Some things could not be made, so her mother took her on a shopping trip to State Street to fill out the rest. Annie would be radiant on her wedding night. Annie's shower was great fun and Brian's bachelor party the week before the wedding was a smashing roar; the buddies had to carry Brian up the stairs; he was so drunk. He had to call in sick the next day too. Annie did not understand why Brian had to get so drunk and she told him so. She also explained that he would be very moderate at both the rehearsal dinner and the reception itself. She made it very clear to the best man, Carl, that it was his personal responsibility to act as Brian's conscience.

The wedding was a great success, and in the afternoon they said goodbye to everyone for the long drive to Starved Rock. Annie was very nervous about her wedding night and fidgeted the entire way, making Brian crazy. Halfway there, she confessed to Brian about her nerves. Brian pulled over, held her hands, gave her a huge kiss and assured her that she would be wonderful. The trick, he explained, was to go slow and just enjoy the moment. The advice proved a huge success; Annie discovered that she loved having sex with Brian and found herself eager for rounds two or three (exhausting him). He slept like a log Saturday night with a huge smile on his face. She slept like death and had an even bigger smile on her face. She could not wait for Sunday morning.

The weekend was fabulous; Annie and Brian were animated as hell on the way home, talking constantly about the future. Brian stopped for gas and realized while filling the tank, he had less than six dollars and the gas was already past that amount. He put his head into the car and asked if she had any money; Annie found eight dollars and some change. They feasted on cold ham sandwiches and a bottle of beer before going home. Annie suddenly jerked her head and with a whimsical look on her face asked exactly where home was. Stupidly, Brian realized that in all the chaos not only did they not have an apartment, but that they were lacking furniture as well. They simply never got around to finding some place to live, so they flipped a coin and showed up at the Flynn's flat and asked for refuge, which was gladly granted. Annie in her old room and Brian on the couch.

Since they both had to go to work the next day, Mrs. Flynn stepped up to the plate and called friends and neighbors asking about small apartments. She found several and by Saturday they had a place to live—one bedroom, a bath, tiny kitchen, parlor and eating nook. They spent Saturday shopping at Sears on Lawrence Avenue for a bed and furniture. They were now the proud owners of brand-new, gleaming furniture and a Sears' credit card (and nearly four hundred dollars in debt). Brian's family and the Flynns all contributed odds and ends so that by the middle of the week they could actually make dinner at home. Brian celebrated by drinking too much and it took Annie everything in her power to get him up on time for work. Despite her efforts, she was certain that he missed roll call that morning. Annie brooded the entire day and had stern words for Brian over dinner that night. There would be many more of these conversations as the years went on.

CHAPTER THREE:

Growing up at St. Gertrude

The McAvoy's had two girls within twenty months—not exactly Irish twins, but darn close to it. Three years later The Brother was born, and by 1960 Peeps arrived. By this time they had moved into a two bedroom apartment, and Annie had long ago given up her job to raise children. The grandparents were great, especially the Flynns. They often came to the apartment with a bag or two of groceries and a case of beer. Money was very tight and Annie was in charge of the family finances. Brian handed over his paycheck (minus his bar and bookie bills every week). He did not seem to understand how precarious the finances were. They had a tiny amount saved. Annie did everything she could to make money stretch. She sewed the kids' clothes, made her own drapes, babysat just like in high school to make a buck or two. Because of the kids, she really could not look for part-time work to help out. She fretted about money constantly; she fretted about Brian even more.

Brian hated to go to work and seemed incapable of *not* drinking. He had an inexplicable need to be with his buddies after work, which meant the tavern (which meant drinking). It was increasingly difficult to get him off to work in the morning. And as a result of monthly shift changes, his work and drinking schedules butted heads. While Brian clearly had a problem, Annie knew of other police families who had it much worse. Brian did take an interest in his kids when they were younger; as they got older, however, he rarely had time or interest in spending any time with them at all. The one thing that Brian never did was treat the family poorly; he never hit his kids or took out his frustrations on Annie. Aside from Brian's booze, their other problem was that the family needed more space. Annie really wanted a house. Apartment living was crowded and noisy. Her kids were loud and so was everyone else's. Morning bathroom call was chaos—six people and one bathroom. The Sisters always got in first and took forever to get ready (no matter how often the others pounded on the door). The Brother and the Old Man got to the point that they would go out to the alley to piss—that was how desperate they became. How she was going to get that dream of a house with three bedrooms, she had no idea. It seemed like a financial daydream.

Brian's buddy at the Summerdale Station was Emmet. He had the exact same schedule as Brian and they became fast friends. Emmet was married with two kids and in the same financial bind as Brian. They were both frustrated by life in general and work in particular. Emmet was a mirror image of Brian—tall with good looks, and the same bad habits. Annie liked Emmet, but was nervous that the two together would reinforce each other's drinking and gambling. Emmet, however, was a bit of a go-getter. He approached Brian about taking on painting and small home repair jobs on their days off. They would split the money in half. Emmet, it turned out, was also rather talented. He knew how to do this kind of work. Brian was an eager student and a quick learner. Emmet emphasized quality—taking the extra time to scrape, prime and paint carefully. He was emphatic about cleanliness, during and after the job.

With business cards printed, the new E & B Painting Company was formed. Annie and the kids plastered the neighborhoods with business cards: on every bulletin board, at hardware stores, and in mailboxes of homes and apartment buildings. Their first job was for their Captain who lived in St. Hilary parish. The pay was a modest thirty dollars and they were scrupulous and finished the job in a few hours. A beer and three tens sealed the deal. With winter fast approaching, they worked hard at getting inside work. A small porch for a small amount was not going to make anyone rich. A big break came when a neighbor that they did not know asked them to paint the living and dining room of his first floor in the two-flat he shared with relatives. The owner explained that he was getting older and could no longer do the work. Even with the new water-based paints that were just coming on the market, Emmet knew it would be a big job. Pictures had to be taken down, furniture moved and covered and cracks repaired. They bid eighty dollars and completed the work in two days.

Both were exhausted after work so they went to Cine Liquors on Devon for some beers. After four hours at the bar and several rounds of shots, the two men were so liquored up they could barely walk. Brian spent twenty dollars with Mike Booke, the bookie in residence. By the time he walked home, he was so drunk that Annie could barely get him up the stairs. With children crying, she got him to the couch to sleep it off. He rolled off from the couch to the floor and the contents of his pants spilled out. Brian had less than four dollars left from his share. Annie sent the kids to their rooms and sat down and cried. That forty dollars were already spent; the Sears account was due, tuition was two months past due, and the phone bill was a month in arrears. She sat down and cried for nearly twenty minutes. And then she got angry.

She noticed in the pile of crap that came out of Brian's pocket, betting slips from the Cine. Brian kept mumbling that he had the best day of his life. Annie thought at first that it was because of the success of the day's work. Staring at the slips, she wondered if Brian had actually won for a change. Brian never won and this would be his best day ever. She called her mother to watch the kids and walked over to the tavern. When she walked in, all of the men around the bar turned to look. She felt extremely self-conscious, but worked up her courage and walked over to Mike Booke, who was sitting at his usual spot, phone in hand. She told him that she came for her husband's winnings. Booke put her off; Annie started to get really pissed and raised her voice to demand the money. Booke offered a hundred dollars; she said no. He raised it to two. Brian's friend was sitting behind Booke and kept slowly shaking his head as the offer went from five hundred to seven hundred. She was almost in a panic, weak in the knees, as Booke settled for thirteen hundred dollars in cash. Two of Brian's copper buddies offered to walk her home to make sure she was safe.

Now she really cried. She told her mother the entire story. And then the children woke up and they started crying because they were unsure why the ladies were crying. Meanwhile, Brian slept on. Mother and daughter made a solemn pledge to never disclose the source of this money. She had never lied to Brian before. On the other hand, she never had this much money in cash in her life. She took the money to the Devon Bank and deposited the stash into the savings account. The clerk gave her a strange look and Annie looked her straight in the face and told her in no uncertain terms to mind her own business. She had never been so rude to anyone in her life. She just did not care. This was a chance of a lifetime—to have the down payment for a house. She would protect her stash like a wildcat.

In the future, Annie would take charge of all business money (even if it meant showing up her husband in front of a customer). She would be there when the guys got paid. Brian would get five dollars to go to the tavern and she would use the rest to keep their household fluid. Because she was home during the day with the kids, Annie would take the business calls and schedule appointments for Emmet to bid jobs. Brian had no choice but to accept the new realities that Annie was in charge of the business. In mid-May, Annie got a call from Old Mrs. Raynor, as she was called, who lived in a huge house on Hood Street in St. Gertrude parish. It would be the call of a lifetime.

Emmet bid one hundred and fifty dollars to repair and paint the front and back porches. Mrs. Raynor accepted on the spot. Mrs. R. was going to sell the house eventually, say in a year or so she told Emmet. If the guys worked out, they could paint the entire house, inside and out. Emmet and Brian were ecstatic and Annie just could not believe their luck. She reminded her guys, as she referred to them, that they would be working long hours on their days off for months. They could not drink and work. They had to show up on time. She did not remind them that their work had to be top-drawer. It would be. Mrs. Raynor agreed to pay as the work was completed; she knew they needed the money and could not afford to wait two months to be paid. Both guys had vacation days coming and they spent them with Old Mrs. Raynor.

Annie screwed up her courage and called Mrs. Raynor and essentially asked that she take Brian's share personally when pay days came about. The old lady was no fool and she knew what was going on. She simply said yes and would call when she paid for work completed. She explained, in so many words, that she had family who had problems and it was very common. No one seemed to be the slightest bit embarrassed by the arrangement—except Brian. But he got over it. Annie made a special effort to put the kids to bed early, make a great meal, and suggest with a wink and a smile that they go to bed early. A just reward for a hard-working husband. She never got tired of seeing Brian naked and ready to go.

Old Mrs. Raynor called two weeks later to say it was payday. The guys had repaired and painted the entire second floor and she was thrilled with the work. For some reason, she mentioned that the small stucco house east of hers was for sale. The gentleman was a widower and moved to the Admiral, a retirement home on Foster by the lake. She told Annie that the house would sell at a very reasonable price, perhaps as little as thirteen or fourteen thousand dollars. Annie was lit; she asked Mrs. R. if she would make introductions to see the house. She carefully explained to Brian that she had been saving money and they had the five or six hundred dollars for the down payment. Brian could not figure this out. Why had he been working his ass off if they had money. Carefully and with tact, so as to avoid a huge uproar, she explained her hope for a house, that instead of paying rent to make others rich, they could own and build equity in their own home. Brian shrugged; he wanted a beer and told her whatever she wanted was fine with him.

What Brian did not expect was to be dragged out of bed on the last day of his vacation. First they toured the Hood Street house, asking Emmet if he would come along as another set of practiced eyes. Annie was delighted with the three bedroom, one and one-half bath house. It had a huge paneled basement that the kids could use as a playroom. Emmet and Brian spent at least half an hour in conference, debating this and that. Annie had her heart in her throat, fearing they would find something terrible. The house needed work; the stucco painted, kitchen modernized and every room redone. The hardwood floors were perfect,

31

all the rooms had been carpeted for decades. The three huddled for ten minutes and came outside to offer thirteen thousand. The owners wanted five hundred more. Brian tried to appear offended, but knew Annie wanted the house and shook on the deal. Next he had to dress up and go and suck up to the banker at the Devon Bank. Annie had made an appointment with Mr. Sheldon, from the mortgage department.

In point of fact, both were terrified and Mr. Sheldon, cold fish that he was, made no effort to make them comfortable. First they got a lecture for twenty minutes about the responsibilities of home ownership. Then he questioned their ability to pay, reminding them that the sixty dollar mortgage payment did not include taxes and insurance. Brian wanted to get up and deck the guy. Finally, they got down to business; yes, they had been bank customers for many years and never bounced a check. He agreed that they had the down payment. Annie patiently explained that she had been saving for a long time. The snob never bothered to check that most of the money in their savings account was deposited in one visit to the bank. Annie was relieved.

They spent the next hour filling out an application and made copies of taxes and pay stubs that she was told to bring. She also showed her most recent Sears bill, that it was modest and up to date. The old bore spent the next half hour explaining that the mortgage payment was an estimate, they had to make sure that enough was paid to cover insurance and taxes. Annie agreed, as a condition to the mortgage, to buy a consumer loan insurance policy, the proceeds of which would pay off the house in the event that Brian died or was disabled. Brian thought it was a waste of five dollars a month. Sheldon insisted and Annie actually agreed. God forbid, if anything happened to Brian; she and the kids would be out on the street. Sheldon informed them that everything was in order and that the application would go before the loan committee. They would get a letter in thirty days. He promptly got up and without a word left the room.

Annie's mother was watching the kids and she was nervous about being gone so long. Brian insisted that they go to the Cine to celebrate. Annie went for one beer; she knew Brian had some money so she took the car home so he would not drive. She told grandmother and her kids all about the day and everyone went to Walgreens' soda fountain for a treat. Four hours later Brian came home mumbling about how cheap Annie was and how he never had enough money. He fell asleep on the couch, pretending to watch The Lawrence Welk Show. The kids groaned and every time they tried to change the channel, the Old Man woke up and demanded his show. Annie was preoccupied with whether he would get up on time his first day of work after furlough. She feared he was back to his old habits; while working so much at his part-time job, he was too tired to goof off at the tavern, except for a beer or two. Tonight he had to start the midnight shift, which meant showering, shaving and on his way by eleven-thirty. It would be a long evening, but she would get him up no matter what.

Three days after the handshake meeting on Hood, a certified letter arrived from a law firm in the Prudential building. Annie was paralyzed with emotion; she could not open the envelope. She was thrilled and terrified at the same time. No one she knew owned their own house at this time in life. She found three copies of a standard real estate sales contract, describing what was being sold and under what conditions. She read and reread the document four times; she understood most of it. The problem was that they needed someone, a lawyer, to read and dissect the document to make sure it represented what they had all agreed. She called Mrs. Schmidt whose son had just finished law school and was studying for the bar exam. Curtains, blinds, shades, yard tools, including a gas mower were included in the deal. Annie asked the lawyer-to-be to add the dining room table and chairs, just to see what they would say.

Young Schmidt offered to drop off the signed docs on his way to the university the next day. Before signing, Brian asked a surprising number of good questions. What happens if they found major problems, like the furnace did not work or there was a roofing problem? The lawyer explained that the sale was as is. Warts and all, they would have no chance to renegotiate. Was the low selling price meant to entice buyers, regardless of condition? How soon could they move in? What about the taxes; who paid them as they were due in two months? Satisfied with the answers, he smiled at Annie and congratulated her on a great find. They would be very happy in this house. He gave her a huge hug and kiss and sealed the deal with shots and a beer. Young Schmidt found the idea of a cold beer very appealing.

All four kids sat around the dining room table watching their parents buy a house. They were so excited they could hardly contain themselves. Both The Sisters and The Brother would have to change schools, to St. Gertrude. They were scared about the change and talked nervously about leaving their friends. What happens if they did not make new ones? Would they like the school? Could they walk to school like they do now? Peeps was excited because everyone else was excited. He did not start school for a while. He just wanted to know if he could bring his blanket and toys with him. In a panic, he started to cry and only after much hugging and reassurance that everything would go with him, was he satisfied. And he was hungry and it was time for dinner. As a treat, Brian offered to pick up pizza and Pepsi which made him the most popular person in the room.

Now they had to wait for the bank. Annie tried calling about a decision but was told in no uncertain terms that the decision would be made when the loan committee made up its collective mind and not a minute sooner. She did not need to call again. Brian for his part, with some badgering from Annie, began to line up three or four friends to help with the move. Emmet volunteered his cargo van and since they did not own that much, Brian figured it would not take too many trips down Devon Avenue to move everything. Annie went into speed mode, cleaning closets and giving away to the Salvation Army anything of value. She started to make daily trips to the grocery store to collect boxes for packing. Peeps had a great time playing in the boxes and managed to trash one in three. Annie put a stop to that. Her father took some time off from work to help run errands and in general assist in organizing the household for the move. Because they had not told the landlord they were moving, Annie was careful to not draw a lot of attention. The landlords were Hungarian Jews who survived the camps. They were always fair and Annie did not want to cause a problem. She was sure that they could rent the apartment for more than what the McAvoys paid. They spoke little English and reflected the changing ethnic mix of West Rogers Park. Fewer and fewer Germans and Irish and more and more refugee Jews.

The contract came back signed and Annie was ecstatic that it included the dining furniture. Now all they needed was for the bank to come through. After Brian got up for the day, Annie found him sullen and darn right rude. He was curt and seemed uninterested about anything except going to the tavern and drinking with his friends. He even tried to get out of the side job that Emmet had set up for the following Tuesday, their day off. Annie put her foot down, which only made Brian pissier. The children sensed the icy mood and did their best to be out of the house and with their friends. Peeps could not escape. He often sat on his father's lap, arm wrestled and in general made mischief. Brian had become attached to his son and usually had ten or fifteen minutes before dinner. He even got sips of beer. Brian was rough with him and Peeps went crying to his mother. He did not understand why his father turned on him and stayed away for almost a week, preferring to watch cartoons to spending time in the kitchen.

The good news was that the bank gave them the loan; the bad news was that this seemed to set Brian off even more. He came home late, missing dinner but demanding beer. He yelled at the kids and Annie even more. Nothing would please him. Finally, on a Sunday night Annie and Brian had a fight like never before. She demanded to know what was going on, why he was so temperamental. She yelled and he yelled even louder. The kids were both terrified and crying. The neighbors complained—twice—and threatened to call the cops. Brian refused to sign the bank papers. Annie went into a rage and demanded to know why. She threw his beer down the drain and refused to allow him to leave the room, ostensibly to go to the tavern—which was closed on Sunday evening. Everything she worked and planned for months would go up in flames. Finally, in sheer exhaustion Brian blurted out that he was scared about owning this house and all the responsibility that went with it. He felt trapped by the money and the work the house needed. Annie called Emmet for help; he was having his own problems but showed up fifteen minutes later. Annie left the kitchen, closed the door and went to reassure the children. It took a while to calm them but soon everyone was in bed sound asleep.

An hour later, Emmet called to say goodbye, leaving through the back door. Annie found the bank documents signed and dated. She simply said nothing but gave Brian a goodnight kiss and went to bed. She called the bank the next morning and set a time to close the sale. Brian had to take time from work to make the meeting, but at least he stopped the childish pouting and moaning. In fact, he seemed animated and talked to Annie about which rooms they should tackle, how much money they had for repairs and furniture. The Sears account would be stretched to the max in the next few months, but Annie reasoned that was what it was for. Because they were good customers Sears increased their credit line—and just in time. It would take them years to pay it down, if ever, but they had a house to fill up.

Holding the keys in her hand, Old Mrs. Raynor called from her front porch to welcome them and remind Brian that she still had work to be done. The side business had been neglected just a bit and it was absolutely time to get it back on track. Brian quietly groaned at the thought of more work; the house would be a pain-in-the-ass effort just by itself. Resigned, he took the keys and led the troops into the house. The first fight was over bedrooms. The Sisters thought they should have the largest room; they did not get it. All the kids ran for the basement door to explore the paneled rumpus room. They were thrilled. The amount of room for toys, games, friends and just hanging out was huge. The one minor item was that there was no furniture. Somehow they thought that what was down there would be there after the sale. Upset they rumbled upstairs to ask Annie about this and she explained patiently that it just did not work that way. She would find furniture soon enough. In fact, the next day Mrs. Raynor offered an older but serviceable couch and coffee table. It was a start. Today was moving day, so the kids spent the day with their grandmothers. Annie was shocked that it took only three hours to move all of the furniture and boxes. There was not much to show for nearly eleven years of marriage. Annie became a whirling dervish, unpacking boxes, cleaning and setting up bedrooms. She had called all of the utilities this morning, so by the end of the day they had electricity. Gas and phone would follow.

Brian took the Boys to the tavern for sandwiches and beers. When he returned, he went to the garage and found a grill, complete with charcoal and lighter fluid. Hamburgers grilled by Chef Brian were the fare for the day. Peeps came out to watch and advise as Brian started the fire and grilled. Being a novice, he put too much fluid on the charcoal; the flame was enormous and made Peeps cry. Brian laughed and ruffled his hair to tell him it was okay. Some burgers were too well done, others too rare. A few of the buns had burnt marks. With some chips and milk, the meal was a feast. Brian got two rounds of cheers for dinner. He laughed like he had not in years. The Old Man enjoyed this grilling business.

School started in three days and Peeps was the only one at home with Annie, who was increasingly being called Nanna. No one remembers when it started; perhaps one of The Sisters could not pronounce Annie and something like Nanna came out instead. Peeps loved being at home with his mother. It was safe, fun and comforting to be with her. In point of fact, even Peeps admitted that he was a mama's boy, aged four or forty. The Sisters and Brother teased him constantly; he did not care. It was what it was. At four, who understands these things or cares about them. Nanna needed lots of furniture, pictures, and other basics. After six months, the kids' clothes were still stored in some very pretty plastic tubs. Peeps found an old wagon in the alley and mother and son spent two afternoons cleaning, painting and oiling the old buggy. Peeps was thrilled, especially when Nanna did the pulling and he did the sitting. The wagon was a godsend for trolling through yard sales and thrift shops, many of which were clustered on Clark, south in the old Swedish neighborhood called Anderson-ville. Nanna found a preschool program for Peeps hoping that this would help in what she expected to be a difficult transition to kindergarten come the fall. Peeps loved it; he was one of the bigger kids and made friends easily. Nanna had time to plan and plot.

After a couple of weeks of serious seduction, Nanna convinced her husband it was time to get the part-time business up and going again. Brian had only one or two jobs, one of which he was two hours late for and smelled of beer. Emmet agreed this was an issue which needed correcting, although he too was having some serious problems with life and marriage. He had moved out and lived above a deli in an illegal apartment; he was broke and depressed. He spent many evenings at the McAvoys, often for dinner. He frequently fell asleep on the couch and made it difficult for the kids to watch television or just play games. Increasingly they gravitated to the basement when Uncle Emmet was around. Emmet was a bad influence on Brian and Brian on him. It would take all of Nanna's diplomacy to navigate this mess. Surprisingly, Brian took the lead and told Emmet he was welcome for dinner on Tuesdays and Sundays. There were no hard feelings; she owed Emmet a lot and did not want to hurt him.

A month after Easter and the great vomit caper, Emmet missed work for the second day in a row. He did not have a phone and his wife had not heard from him for weeks. Brian and a couple of The Boys from the Cine went looking for his car and for him. The car they found; Emmet they did not. Early in the evening, they went to the deli to talk to the owner who both pretended not to speak English and also denied that he had an illegal apartment upstairs. The storekeeper was a crude little man who grunted rather than spoke, half in English and in an Eastern European language the cops had never heard before. The men were growing impatient with the store owner who was sweating so profusely he had to keep mopping his face and brow with his apron. After ten minutes of bullshit, Brian grabbed him by the shirt collar and told him that they were going up stairs, so get the fuckin' key. They had to move boxes and junk in the hallway just to get to the door. As they opened the door, the smell was overwhelming. Emmet was hanging from a steam pipe. He had been dead for days.

For months, the McAvoy family was distraught. Everyone was depressed and the children just did not understand what had happened. Nanna worked overtime to keep the children close, answer their questions and focus them on the good things in life. Peeps did not understand why Uncle Emmet had not come over; he thought it was his fault. He cried at the drop of a hat. There was no wake, a very unusual happening for an Irish family. There just was no money. The union paid for the casket and burial plot; because he committed suicide there would be no funeral mass. Suicide was a mortal sin of despair for which there was no forgiveness. Brian was enraged by this thinking; he vowed never to set foot in St. Gertrude again. The priest did come to perform a graveside service and a least a hundred officers and their wives attended. For obvious reasons, the only children there were Emmet's two daughters.

Peeps did not want to attend his preschool, and had a royal hissy fit when Nanna tried to coax him into going. After a few days, he began to miss his friends and eventually got back to his routine. He had a problem at school; one that would follow him throughout his life: He refused to answer to his given name, Andrew. He would not speak when spoken to; refused to look up and simply stared into empty space. The teacher did not want to call him Peeps; what kind of a name was that? These Irish were very peculiar people to name a kid after Easter candy. They were clannish and they drank too much. Their kids came to school in rags and looked like they had not been fed in a week. Mrs. Greene was sick of them; she had two years to retire and could not wait.

Nanna thought that for the most part, the summer program for Peeps was a success. The transition to full day kindergarten should be a breeze; except for some crying at the school door, all went well. The name business reared its ugly head again; Sister Mary Agnes was not going to call him Peeps. But the boy acted the same way as with Mrs. Greene; he simply would not respond, not look up and would not move. Sister was crazed; threats, kindness and gentle cajoling did nothing. He would only respond when addressed as Peeps. Nanna came to school to try to help and left defeated. A stubborn five-year-old boy was winning and two adults, three when you add the principal, could not get him to change. After two weeks of this nonsense, Sister gave up and called him Peeps and the boy came alive. She found him fun, responsive and eager to learn.

Peeps thrived in the early years at St. Gertrude. He found four or five boys early on and they were inseparable throughout grade school. As he grew older new kids came to the school and four of them became part of Peeps' gang. Peeps was always tall for his age, a bit clunky in sports and games, and generally made decent grades. He often compared himself to The Brother, three years older. He was one of those kids that had it all: good looking, athletic, very popular, and an excellent student. There were times when Peeps wanted to strangle him. He could never match up to The Brother, and gave up trying. The Brother's huge flaw was that he was embarrassed by his family. All of his friends lived in bigger houses, had fathers with much better jobs, went to Wisconsin for two weeks in the summer and generally had every advantage life could offer. The Brother spent as much time as possible away from home and never invited friends to his house. He also had little time for Peeps.

Peeps' life changed forever mid-way through the sixth grade. Hair started growing under his armpits and he would wake up in the middle of the night with this strange feeling from his dick. He had no idea what was going on and he had no one to talk to. He heard that the priest came in the class to talk to the boys at the end of eighth grade. Big help that would be for Peeps. The Old Man was not someone you went to with these kinds of things; he was preoccupied with his own problems and the Irish never talked about sex—never. He tried to ask The Brother, but was told to figure it out. His friends were no good; they had not started changing yet. But he did learn the joy of playing with himself and, of course, having to go to confession every Saturday so he could take commu-nion on Sunday. It was an exciting, scary and strange time in his life. By seventh grade several of the boys were also changing, and dicks, breasts and girls were the constant conversation among them. One friend, Bobby Mueller, was not Irish and his father talked to him about sex and girls and babies. Bobby passed along everything he was told and even showed the guys a booklet, complete with drawings, all about puberty and sex. By the eighth grade Peeps thought he could give the sex class better than the priest. He would use the words everyone understood instead of all the technical garbage.

When he was much older, he would get furious when one of the drunks at the Bubble would start complaining about the nuns, that they all had rulers and smacked you whenever they had a chance. It was just not true; such talk was an urban myth that every nun was a monster. The Sisters of the Blessed Virgin Mary, all twelve of them who ran St. Gertrude, had never hit a student. Peeps had never seen it nor heard of anything like that. They ran a tight ship, they had to. There were over one thousand kids in the school, with huge numbers in each classroom. Everyone in school disliked some teachers; you could not help it. That was what kids did—complain about teachers, homework and discipline.

Seventh and eighth grades were a total blur. Peeps loved every girl in school. But he was on the shy side and just a little too big for his age. He was shaving by the middle of eight grade and spent every minute of his free time playing basketball. He desperately wanted to make the eighth grade boys team; he would never match his brother who was the star of a very good team. Peeps was lucky to make a basket or two each game, grab a few rebounds, and try not to foul out—which he did with some regularity. The team was average; they finished in fourth place in two tournaments; at least they were able to bring some hardware home for the school trophy case.

While Peeps was enthralled with eighth grade and the world in general, Nanna and the Old Man were preoccupied with money and high school tuitions. Nanna had found a job at the local department store. The Old Man mocked how little she made, but she just ignored him. His drinking was getting worse and she was terrified that he would lose his job. On top of it, there was a huge police scandal at the Summerdale station, where the old man worked. Indictments and firings spread across the front pages of newspapers almost daily. Each officer had to undergo a mandatory lie detector test or lose his job immediately. There was not an officer at the station who had not taken something at some time. But they were not after the petty stuff; they wanted to root out very serious corruption at all levels of the department.

The Old Man was scared shitless. Of course he had taken small gifts for small favors. Everyone did it. No one at the station knew exactly what they were after. The men spent every free moment digesting the latest gossip and rumors. Officers turned on their friends in order to curry favor. The code of silence broke like a shattered store window. The Old Man's reaction to all this was to drink more. Finally, after weeks of small benders Nanna got him to sober up and not drink until the crisis was over. If he lost his job, he would be lucky to be a night watchman at a third of what he was making. Nanna could never pay the mortgage and the rest of the bills on her measly salary. They would have to sell the house, the kids would go to public schools and they would be back in a two bedroom apartment in the blink of an eye.

Peeps was oblivious to the entire scandal; he had just taken the entrance exam for Loyola Academy, and like his friends, was anxiously waiting to hear from the school. Nanna had The Sisters, The Brother and Peeps stay at the table after dinner to explain what was going on. The older kids understood all of it and berated Peeps with being so selfish and stupid. Nanna's talk was very sobering and all the kids walked away scared out of their wits. For the first time in many years, Peeps cried himself to sleep. He was not sure who he felt sorrier for: Nanna or himself. He spent every afternoon after school hanging around the store in the backroom with Nanna when no customers were present. After all he was a mama's boy and he found comfort and reassurance just being with her. Nanna was grateful for his support, even though he was only fourteen years old. Mother and son were in this together.

The Old Man got off easy; he lost one week's pay, a reprimand was placed in his personnel jacket and he was transferred, as further punishment, to a police district on the west side, nearly a forty minute drive each way from home. Not only was the new district far, it was also a crappy part of the city. It was very industrial and very poor, mostly Black and Puerto Rican. Residents hated the white Irish cops and the coppers were not kind to the locals. If the police had a code of silence, the neighborhood had an iron-clad one. No one, absolutely no one would help with a criminal investigation. The Old Man did not understand this at all; if someone did dirt in your grandmother's neighborhood would you not want to get this guy? He sure would, but not so on the west side.

One hot Sunday evening, the Old Man and his partner were idling at the light on west Twenty-sixth street, when a woman came screaming to the car carrying a four year old Hispanic girl. Neither cop could understand what she was saying; they spoke no Spanish. Opening the door and facing the woman, the Old Man realized that the girl was not breathing; she was blue from choking on food. He grabbed the girl, put her over his knees and used the palm of his hand to pound on her back; three or four times he tried, until the food dislodged and she was breathing. By this time, a small crowd had gathered expecting that the Irish cops were harassing someone from the neighborhood. To their surprise, they witnessed the Old Man's quick action and broke out into applause. The English speakers thanked the men profusely and promised to call the station to tell what he had done. Both officers received a citation of valor for their quick action. For just one brief moment, the code of silence was broken. The irony was that just a week before both men were part of a larger group of officers who were trained in CPR. The Old Man thought the training was a waste of time, but he was very happy that he had paid attention to the instructor.

Things returned to normal at the McAvoy household, a mixed blessing if there ever was one. Nanna was having a very hard time getting the Old Man up for work. The kids all helped. All he wanted to do was drink and then sleep it off. His new partner and the other men at the station were great enablers. They covered for him and kept their silence in front of the brass. But the brass knew what was going on; this kind of problem was rampant throughout the police department. There was no program for mental health services, the kinds of things that would have helped both Emmet and the Old Man. Each had needs and the department did not see itself in the social services business. The men would just have to tough it out.

For Peeps, life could not be better. He had a girlfriend named Linda, he was one of the four captains of an intramural basketball league that played every Thursday after school. His team went undefeated over the nine games but lost in the finals to one of his best friends. He was mortified and pissed and did not talk to Roger for a week. Roger was the type not to notice anyway. There were dances at various schools in the area and parties. The McAvoys had two of them in a recently refurbished basement rec room, thanks to Nanna's superb efforts. The parties were a blast. Twenty or so boys and girls would dance, laugh, listen to music and make out if they could. The Sisters were the chaperones and they did not put up with nonsense. No dirty dancing; you had to leave room for the Holy Ghost when slow dancing. That left every boy in the room very frustrated and not a few of the girls as well. Some certainly were not going to save it for marriage. Peeps was convinced that he would die a virgin at this rate. To top it off, he and all his friends were accepted to Loyola. What a wonderful life.

The wonderful life crashed in a matter of weeks. The Old Man was sound asleep in his car, not an unusual event the neighbors noted. This time he was not passed out; Nanna could not raise him and get him to respond to her. Hysterical, she called 911 and waited for an ambulance, which seemed to take forever. The paramedics rushed him to Edgewater Hospital, the nearest trauma center, and he was admitted to the intensive care unit. He stayed in a coma for nearly two weeks and died quietly on Good Friday. The kids were not allowed to see him; you had to be eighteen. When told that the Old Man had died, Peeps could not find it in him to cry. He was such a distant man, always preoccupied by his own problems, especially the last few years.

The wake went on for two nights; the Irish made wakes into a sporting event. The affair took place at Maloney's on Devon and Glenwood, conveniently located across the street from a local watering hole, the Glenway Inn. There was no weeping and gnashing of teeth. No one was surprised that he died of the drink. But there was great sympathy for Nanna and the kids. How would they manage? What would the kids do about high school? Everyone knew that they lived from paycheck to paycheck—most of them did also. What about the house, people mused. How could they keep it? Nanna thanked God that she had insisted on the loan insurance in case something happened to Brian. She would own the house free and clear. These were not exactly warm and sentimental thoughts at the time of her husband's death; then again they had not been close for the last seven or eight years. Each of them were preoccupied with their own concerns and issues. Life at the McAvoy house was grim and all business. They were consumed by survival, nothing more.

After Mass and burial, friends and neighbors came to the house. The place was full of food and booze; neighbors arranged everything, a tradition in their part of the city. The affair went on for hours, with increasingly loud laughing and storytelling, fueled by booze. Nanna and the kids had to literally kick the last of the well-wishers out the front door. The Brother became increasingly abusive to everyone. Secretly he hated his father and did not much like his family either. When he went to college it would be far away. He was determined to get away from these people, family and neighbors included. He had one more year at Loyola Academy and was assured by his college counselor he would get many offers for full scholarships; there certainly was no family money to screw up the works. He felt as poor as some kid from the ghetto. Maybe he was that kid from the ghetto.

The following week Nanna was in a whirlwind of paperwork and phone calls. She had to submit death certificates and fill out forms for Social Security, the police pension board, the life insurance company, the bank and its insurance company for the house and seek financial relief for one of her girls from St. Scholastica. Mr. Maloney's bill had to be paid, so she took out what they had in savings, anticipating the future death payment of five thousand dollars. She spent time explaining to the three older children that they were on their own for college; they would have to find scholarship money or work part time and go to school part time. Because Peeps was not yet a student at Loyola, Father's Club offered no help with tuition; she appealed to the school, but was told that there was nothing that could be done. Those were the rules. She could help Peeps for the first two years, but he would have to make the full three hundred dollars for his junior and senior years. Everyone understood except The Brother. He just stormed out swearing at no one in particular.

CHAPTER FOUR:

Loyola Academy — give us a boy and we will give you a man

For Peeps, the summer after eighth grade graduation was fantastic. He was gifted nearly one hundred and fifty dollars, most of which went directly to Nanna for the school bus to Wilmette, and for books. He dogged the neighborhood looking for grass-cutting jobs and managed to make ten dollars a week. This kept him flush for dates, movies and records. He felt up his first girl, but he could not brag too much about it; he was sure that all of his friends had taken her to the back row of the Granada Theater. At least he was making progress to being a man. Evenings at the Thorndale beach were particularly fun, as it was a blistering summer. Nanna was preoccupied with work and managing the household after the Old Man's death. She put few limits on him; she knew he and his friends did not get into much trouble. Next on the list for Peeps' gang was beer and smoking some grass. But these would have to wait.

The summer ended with a thud; the first day of school was orientation day. Students were herded into homerooms, given class schedules, told the rules about what to wear, silence in the corridors, being late for school, jug, and assorted other items. They were assigned a locker with a combination lock and a locker mate. They went to the gym to buy books, phys-ed clothes, a jock and a Speedo for the pool. They were assigned a cubicle for gym clothes in the

47

locker room. It was so small the clothes never dried and the towel smelled like chicken shit after the first week. They were instructed very sternly by the coaches to take the towel home every Friday and bring a fresh one every Monday. Almost everyone changed their towels at Christmas and Easter breaks. It was a boys' school and strong, pungent smells were part of its charm.

The next day, Friday, was a school day but they were let out early. The school celebrated the Mass of the Holy Spirit, a long-standing and venerable Jesuit tradition. The school community was assembled to pray to the Holy Spirit for inspiration and knowledge—for success in their studies. It was a big deal; all sixteen hundred boys covered the gym floor; parents and faculty packed the balcony of the gym. Fifteen priests concelebrated the mass; there was a choir, the band played and led the singing of hymns throughout the service. It took an hour and a half to finish and it was sweltering; Peeps could not keep his mind on the events from the heat and the fact that he had a raging hard on the entire time. He thought seriously about skipping communion rather than walk up in front of thousands with a huge bulge in his pants. Good grief what a way to start, he thought.

Each morning Peeps' gang waited for the school bus to Wilmette; they were the first on and last off. Each morning The Brother and friends drove by in relative comfort, giving them the finger, calling them frosh assholes and mocking them with great enthusiasm. The seniors never tired of humiliating the freshman. What made it worse was the fact that there was room in the car for Peeps. The Brother never offered and he lied to Nanna that there was no room in the car. He could care less that the ride would have saved a hundred dollars. He wanted nothing to do with Peeps.

The routine of high school fell on Peeps like a great blanket; nothing ever changed. He had classes in Latin, History, English, Algebra, Religion and Phys Ed plus a homeroom in which to conduct the business of going to high school. Announcements, tickets for dances and football games, collections for the conversion of pagan babies and assorted bullshit were covered during that period. He would be in the same homeroom for four years and in the end hardly knew any of the other guys. Peeps did not seem to care, neither did the rest of them. Everyone seemed to belong to a group or clique—kids you grew up with, jocks, debaters, Torch Club, like that. It was not until senior year that these barriers came down; everyone seemed to grow up at the same time, talking about who the easy girls were, sports, dances, college plans and just growing up. Peeps found, and made, some amazing friends he earlier would have avoided as though they had the plague. Years later he regretted being so provincial and shy. What a colossal blunder.

Before the end of freshman year, all the boys participated in the annual retreat. Classes were suspended for two days to make time for the Reverend Herbert J. Ratterman, S.J., the retreat master. His specialty was sex and sin geared for fifteen year olds. And he was a piece of work. He could thunder damnation, tell very funny stories about boys and their dicks. There were Bible readings, sermons, confession devoted specifically to impure thoughts and beating off. No part of the two days was left to anything else except sex. He learned more sins than he could ever imagine. By the end of the first day, Peeps and everyone at the lunch table were sick of it. They were tired of feeling like pond-scum sinners; they were sick of stories about hell and eternal damnation because you jacked off and died before you got to confession. Personally, Peeps was beginning to rethink the whole sex and hell crap.

He decided to test his ideas on Fr. Kramer, who taught seniors. He went to confession before class and tallied up his usual number of sex sins; he then ask father if killing a man was a mortal sin. Of course, came the reply; why do you ask. Peeps wanted to know how killing someone and masturbating could both be mortal sins. God certainly would condemn the unrepentant murderer to hell; would He really send a kid to hell for all eternity for having dirty thoughts? Peeps did not think God would do that and told Fr. Kramer so. The priest thought a minute and said he did not think God would do that to a kid either. Peeps shared his confession with his mates at lunch; some guys were shocked, others had that knowing look on their faces as they listened to Peeps. Peeps solved the conundrum very easily: He stopped taking communion and continued on his merry way to becoming a man, as he saw it.

On the home front, the family settled into a domestic pattern without shouting and chaos. Since the Old Man had died, the household was pleasant and a nice place to bring friends. The Sisters were both enrolled at the two year college for women, Mundelein College, literally on the Loyola University campus. They worked part-time and took classes in the morning; just about everything they earned went to pay tuition and books. Nanna helped a bit. The real truth of the matter was that they spent most of their time scouting for husbands. They hunted out the North Shore boys particularly, as they had the best prospects. Pre-med and dentistry guys were the best; but they certainly would not turn down a graduating senior in finance or pre-law. They were sly but hungry in their pursuit. They flirted with everyone and unlike their mother's era, sex was an important part of college living. Neither threw themselves at a boy, but if he seemed serious, well, there could be rewards.

Nanna had a new life and Peeps was a big part of it. She was very comfortable with the boy and would talk about finances, the state of the house and her work, normally the kind of thing she would share with the Old Man. She gained confidence and was able to manage her brood with love and kindness. She was promoted to the manager of the ladies' unmentionables department, getting a twenty dollar a week raise as a reward. She was a great sales lady; she was patient and helpful with customers and built up a good following. She learned to manage inventory and buy like a State Street professional. Her department was the most profitable in the store. She was a big fish in a small pond, but secretly relished her new life. She was sad for Brian, but she did not miss him one bit. She had a new life; she went out for drinks with some of the ladies at the store and got the attention of more than one of the salesmen that came to call on her. Flattered by their interest, and two were very persuasive, she put them off. She was not about to get married again. One marriage for a lifetime. Peeps no longer stopped at the store; bras and panties were not part of his image.

The Brother was as unpleasant as a fart in a phone booth. He brooded constantly, liked to drink, lived at his friends' houses and was as rude and curt as he possibly could be. Every McAvoy kid, in turn, took the old man's police shirts, blouses actually, to the Chinaman on Clark Street just north of Thome.

The shirts had so many pleats and had to be starched like a board, so most wives sent the shirts out to be laundered. The only place in the neighborhood who would take them, for a quarter a piece, was the commercial laundry run by two Chinese guys. Even in the middle of January, the windows would be wide open, it was so hot from boiling cauldrons of hot, soapy water. Typically, The Brother refused to take his turn; he did not want his friends to see him walking down the street with laundry and into the Chinaman's. He forced Peeps into volunteering to run the errand by threatening to beat the shit out of him if he did not go each week. The place was really strange: no one spoke English, he never gave his name, yet he always got the right shirts back. One time he did not have the dollar for the shirts, and the Chinaman refused to take the shirts. Peeps pushed the shirts across the counter and he pushed them back. After five minutes of this, Peeps crying like crazy, the Chinaman gave in and took the shirts, no doubt calling him every pig's body part with the f-bomb attached—all in Chinese of course. If The Younger Sister was the queen of bitches and witches, The Brother surely was the prince of dickheads and assholes.

Two months before graduation, The Brother received a full scholarship to Georgetown University in Washington, D.C.; this included books and housing. Georgetown was a real prize and The Bother was certain that he deserved it all. He also found a paying internship downtown at a major accounting firm, thanks to a father of a friend from Wilmette. He did not bother to share either bits of news until one Monday morning he came down with a shirt and tie on. As for graduation itself, the young men were expected to wear a tux for the ceremony. This was a long-standing Loyola tradition. He told his Nanna that she had to dress up for the ceremony, giving her two days to find an acceptable dress. He made it perfectly clear that she needed to look right to fit in.

On the way to graduation, Nanna tried to get him to open up. The Brother would not talk—even about prom night. He drove in sullen silence and was the same on the way home. He hustled her out of the school, barely having a chance to congratulate the neighborhood boys and their parents, people she had known forever. She was completely frozen out and she began to cry silently for the entire ride home. The boy was unmoved and unfazed. Nanna never felt so alone in her entire life. This athlete, this stud, this scholar whom she called her son was emotionally void. This was the last time they spent more than three minutes in the same room for the rest of the summer.

Peeps, without working up a sweat, managed a B-average and received second honors for his efforts. Nanna was pleased; The Sisters mocked him because they knew he did almost nothing to get the grades. Only one class was not a snooze, Algebra taught by a cranky old Jesuit priest who had as much self-control with fifteen year olds as a ninety year old bladder. Peeps was fairly certain that the priest was eighty years old. This was the only class that he really goofed off in; he got jug three or four times that year. Jug, short for the Latin word jugum or ox collar, was a nasty torture that could only have been perfected by a Jesuit mind. You went to a room with fifty other screw offs and you had to memorize the first definition of every word, on both sides of a dictionary page. It was crowded, uncomfortable on the floor—the upperclassmen pushed you out of a desk if you happened to get one—and very hard to concentrate. Roll call was at four and five o'clock. Three or four words were asked; you sat down or came back the next day if you failed. After three days you were released. Then he had to hitchhike home on the Edens Expressway and down Peterson Avenue to get close to home. After his first year, he never got jug again. He hated it. Jug was cruel and unusual punishment and there ought to be a law.

Halfway through the summer of sophomore year, Peeps applied for a part-time job at Dominick's Finer Foods on Broadway. He had to make money, otherwise he would be going to Our Lady of St. Senn, the local public high school; Senn was not exactly an institution of higher learning. He was scared shitless when he went for the application; the head cashier was patient and explained everything. He would take the application home, fill it out, bring a copy of his birth certificate to prove he was sixteen and provide three references from adults who knew him well. He would have to take a test, simple math questions. Nanna edited the application and made him do it over again so it could be read. She marched him down the street to talk to neighbors to be references. Greg and Nancy next door, family friends from forever, were happy to write a letter. The next evening he returned the application and was taken to the break room to take the test. He missed one of the forty questions.

In the meantime he continued to hustle grass-cutting jobs; so far he had only one hundred and ten dollars for the four hundred plus he needed for school. Nanna gave no indication that she would help. He was jittery as hell over the next weeks; he was rude and insolent. Nanna had to put him in his place twice just to keep a civil tongue in his head. He took up swearing under his breath, which made Nanna crazy. Suddenly both her sons were pains in the ass. Boys are a bad lot, she thought—paraphrasing Mr. Dickens. One said nothing, the other said way too much. Relief came for mother and son when the store called and he was hired, but was on probation for the first month. If he were late for work, not dressed correctly, slacked off or screwed around or rude to customers, he would be fired. He made two dollars an hour while on probation and fifty cents more after that. He needed to wear a white shirt and clean tie; blue jeans were alright. He was to be at the store one-half-hour early the first Saturday. He bagged groceries, helped take bags to cars if customers needed help and made sure the parking lot was cleared of carts. He learned the trick to double bagging, how to push five or six carts back into the store without breaking a window and most importantly how to say thank you to customers. By the time he got home, he was too tired to even eat. He wanted a shower and watched television. He was on the schedule for the next three Saturdays; so far he had not been yelled at so he thought the day went well. At this rate, he could easily make fifty dollars a month. He would even have some spending money. Secretly Nanna was very proud of him.

After two weeks, he fell in love with one of the part-time cashiers, only to find out that she was twenty and in college. Well that was not going to work. Thank God he never asked her out; what a pile of shit that would have been. He thought it better to stick around home and school for a girl. On a whim, he called up Linda Ney, a girl with whom he had gone to grade school and who now went to St. Scholastica. They went to the movies a few times, made out in front of her parents' house, joined other friends at dances and the beach in hot weather. Peeps was not sure, but he thought that the Neys had a lot of money.

Linda got a car for her sixteenth birthday; it was not a used junker like Nanna's ride, but a brand new car. He was careful to bring her home on time and her parents took a shine to him, though they thought his name was very peculiar. He was very polite; if they only knew that he wanted to bed their daughter in the back of that brand new car.

There is one universal truth: Summer vacation never lasted nearly as long as it should have. His school schedule arrived in the middle of August: Latin II, Algebra II, Biology, English, Religion and the famous Phys-ed. Dreading school was his major function during the week; he concentrated on work on Saturday. The third Saturday of August was one for the record books. He had planned to go out with some of the older guys to drink some beer and maybe smoke grass. He had not noticed that Nanna and The Sisters were sitting in the darkened living, just staring. He went to his room to get clean clothes and take a shower. He pushed the door open but could barely squeeze in. The room was in rubble: suitcases, clothes, shopping bags and The Brother's personal items. Peeps started to push the junk on the floor so he could sit down on his bed. The Brother grabbed him by the neck and told him not to touch his fucking stuff. He pushed Peeps into the open closet and challenged him to do something about it. The Brother was very drunk and very volatile; Peeps knew he could not take him; The Brother had played four years of football and wrestled for two. After his shower and a parting fuck you to his brother he went out for the evening. He did not smoke grass, but the beers were fun and being part of a group of older guys was a cool item.

Peeps was tired and came home early; he made sure that he had plenty of gum for the walk home so he did not smell like beer. Nanna might still be up; and she was. She stopped him and asked him to sit at the table with her for a few minutes. Nanna explained that the three women were virtual captives while The Brother was raging in his room. It finally ended when he took a shower and fell sound asleep on the floor. Nanna had looked in and turned off the light. She told Peeps she was never more scared in her life. She shared the ride to and from graduation; she wondered if he was already a drunk or drug addict. Was he mentally ill? Could she get him to a doctor? He was eighteen and she had no control over him. Peeps listened and said little. As she got up to go to bed, she told him point blank he was too young to drink. She did not want him to become a mirror image of father and brother.

On Sunday the whole house was up by 7:30. After showering, The Brother was busy dragging four very heavy suitcases to the front door with as much noise and swearing as he could manage. Even though they were still sick of his crap from the night before, they got up. By the time the suitcases had made it to the front porch, a car pulled up and a friend was waiting. The Brother turned, stared at them for a moment, and announced he was leaving for good. He would never come back to this dump and you bunch of losers. Ever. He gave Peeps the finger and told him that he would never be anything but a stupid dickhead. With luggage in tow, he headed to the van, high-fived his friend with a huge smile, packed the car and left. He never looked back. This short drama exhausted all four of them; they went back to bed, saying nothing.

Over the summer Peeps took the driving test and passed. While he rarely asked for the car, he did ask if he could drive to school two days a week. He and two friends would take turns driving and in the course of the year save the hundred dollars the bus would have cost. She agreed but only if he took it over to the garage and had it checked out, rotating the tires, changing the oil and in general making sure it was serviceable. The car was a Covair Manza, which Ralph Nadar called the worst car on the road. It was air cooled with the engine where the trunk should be. It was not much, but it would get him to school. He probably did not save a dime; he did not realize that he had to pay for the additional insurance. It did not matter; he wanted off the bus in the worst way.

Sophomore year was decidedly more difficult than freshman year. The Jesuits really knew how to turn up the screws. Algebra II was a complete mystery. He doubted that he ever got one homework assignment or a single quiz question right; thank God for partial credit and a huge curve. He got a D+ for all four quarters and Peeps was damn happy to get that. The class was the first of the day and he had a very hard time keeping awake; he would rest his head against the wall until it was time to work on the homework problems. The teacher was a real snooze; this was his first teaching job after coming out of the army. He had two suits, one black and the other gray. He wore the black suit one day, the gray the next. Day three it was the black jacket with the gray pants; day four the gray jacket with the black pants. And so it went for the entire year. Hopefully the clothes got to the cleaner during vacations; Peeps was not interested in getting close enough to find out.

Biology was a great class, taught by a young and enthusiastic Jesuit in training. But it was a lot of work. He spent every night memorizing some list or other: bones, phylum, insects and parts of the brain. While not by any means brilliant in the class, he felt a great deal of satisfaction when he managed to keep a solid B throughout the year. And thank the stars for a very smart lab partner who could not find the balls of a male frog. When asked for help, the instructor told him, out loud for the class to hear, that he had a very fine pair of testes. The class roared and the Jesuit scholastic burned with embarrassment for five minutes. His lab partner immediately was named Frog Balls. Peeps and Frog Balls were a great team.

The sophomores had the second lunch period, right after the freshman at eleven thirty. The crowd gathered early to get into the cafeteria. Four hundred were piled at the two doors, supposedly in silence. It was very easy to get a jug for talking and Peeps was careful not to fall into the proctors' net. One day, because they were crammed into the corridor like animals, Peeps started mooing, softly, of course. Seconds later ten or fifteen sophomores did the same. They were sedate, gentle moos, said under the breath. It drove the teachers crazy. There were so many kids, and especially the smaller guys could not be seen. The more the teachers demanded to know who was mooing, the more the noise. The mooing spread to the other door as well; the place was in chaos. When the doors opened, four hundred boys surged into the cafeteria laughing and mooing as they rushed to get into line for lunch. Peeps had his lunch already in a brown paper bag: two sandwiches, two oranges, an apple and a banana. After all, he was a growing boy.

Once in the cafeteria, Peeps' mob pulled two tables together, so that about twenty boys could sit around it. The Jesuit Scholastic who covered that area did not mind that they put the tables together. In addition to the St. Gertrude guys, there were mates from St. Ignatius, St. Henry in the city, and St. Norbert in Northbrook. For whatever reason, this group of city and suburban kids got along extremely well. Besides food and sex, the main conversation was telling Helen Keller jokes. Almost every day, someone had a new one. After all they were sophomores, literally from the Greek for wise fools. A typical joke: How did Helen Keller burn her fingers; she tried reading a waffle iron. Or, mimicking sign language, Helen Keller was trying to call for help from the bottom of a well. And of course the standard: How did Helen Keller fall in the night; the night light was not on. The repertoire kept growing. After a month of this, the Jesuit heard the jokes and took the table to task. Quietly and very effectively, he managed to humiliate each of them individually, and as a group. Many red faces had to apologize for their behavior. They did not get a jug; they just got a serious lesson in humility. Give us a boy and we will give you a man.

The Brother's presence, or lack of, continued to be a pall on the McAvoy household. No one talked about it; everyone was busy with their own lives. Nanna kept her silence for nearly a month, then after dinner asked everyone to stay so she could talk about his leaving. She just could not abandon her son, no matter how poorly he behaved. What really prompted the discussion was a letter that had come to the house. It was addressed to The Brother, but Nanna decided to open it anyway. The letter was to inform him that he had lost his scholarship and other benefits for failure to attend class. He had not gone for even one lecture. He was told that he could reapply next semester, if there was a valid reason for his absence. By the time she stopped reading the letter out loud, Nanna was shaking so hard they had to give her some brandy just to calm herself. Strange behavior now became eerie. What was going on? They had no address or phone number, so they decided to talk to some of the Old Man's friends who were captains and lieutenants. They suggested that the family place a missing person's request with the D. C. police. They would make the first calls and get a name for them to follow up.

Within a week, Nanna received a detailed form in the mail, asking anything and everything about her son: age, height, weight, color of his hair and eyes, noticeable marks, general physical description and everything about the last time he was seen. It was extremely painful to recount their last time together, but she worked at the task resolutely and in as much detail as she could. She asked each of the young people to review her work. Surprisingly Nanna did not have a recent picture of the boy; she cut out the pictures and short biography from the yearbook and included them with the form. She added a personal message to Detective Small of the D.C. police missing persons department thanking him profusely for his help. She added her phone number and told him he could call anytime, day or night. She made copies of everything and reminded the detective that she was a widow of a Chicago police officer. Anything to get him to focus his time and attention on her child.

Nanna spent every free moment writing and calling every person at the university whom she thought might be of help. No one knew him; the wall of silence was deafening. She cried herself to bed every night. Everything about her older boy baffled her; she also became increasingly dependent on Peeps.

Both of The Sisters were now engaged to be married and unfortunately she just could not get motivated to be excited for them. Frankly, it was a relief that The Younger Sister in particular was moving on. For the last three or four years, this girl had been a real pain in the neck. The problem began when she was just starting her junior year in high school. She decided she was grown up and could do what she wanted. Nanna felt she was an immature and undisciplined girl who needed direction and limits. The fight was on. Every weekend she came in late, often smelling of beer. She would try to sneak in after curfew and Nanna got up to confront her. There was always yelling, swearing and door slamming. Every weekend and during summer break she acted out. When she was grounded, she snuck out the bedroom window. When the car was denied, she took it anyway after Nanna went to sleep. Nanna even asked The Older Sister to talk to her. That turned out to be a waste of time. After two years of these rows, she was in college. She actually settled down a bit; The Queen of the Bitches and Witches was finally growing up. It could not happen at a better time. Her engagement seemed to be the settling event in her life.

When not worrying about her son, Nanna was obsessed about paying for two weddings in short order. She went to the bank and took out a small loan on the house and with her savings told the girls what she had to spend. Fortunately, both girls were reasonable (which shocked Nanna) in their expectations and used what savings they had to work out the details. The Sisters explained to their future husbands the facts of life and they and their parents agreed to help out as well. The girls deserved better, at least one of them anyway, thought Nanna; they were mostly good and helped with the house and finances as much as they could. Short of finding gold on Thorndale Beach, there was nothing else to do but enjoy the days and see them off to happy and prosperous lives without any more Saturday night fights on the back porch.

Peeps felt the pressure of his mother's emotional needs. He just did not know what he could do to help her. He was sixteen and screwed up as a soup sandwich. He wanted to hide; he did not care about his brother. In fact, with a beer or two in him, he could only manage cold rage whenever his name came up. He told his girlfriend Linda everything and she was a real good scout, rubbing his back and encouraging him not to get down. Peeps was increasingly physically attracted to Linda. She was long and lean and liked to make out as much as he did. He was positive that he could get her into bed eventually. In the meantime, he was left to his own increasingly dirty thoughts and his own private goings on. One bright light: He got an A in Latin; he loved *Caesar's Gallic Wars*.

The shit hit the fan on the Friday before Christmas break. Detective Small called in the early evening to tell Nanna that they had found her son. He was dead from a drug overdose and was buried in a Potter's field in Maryland. He was found about ten blocks from the White House, in a very seedy part of town. The coroner had conducted a full autopsy complete with urine and blood tests. Pictures and physical matches to a tee. Randy McAvoy died alone, drugged up and with no one to mourn him. The police did not find his clothes, suitcases, money or identification. Nanna was in complete denial; Peeps so confused he did not know what to think or say; The Sisters held Nanna and cried violently. How could this happen to a man with such promise: the looks, the brains and the athletic skills. When talk started about moving the body to Chicago, The Sisters put their foot down. There was no money and he did not deserve the dignity of a family funeral. He was lost to them. Detective Small filed his final report and sent a copy to Nanna with a note of condolence. The case of Randy McAvoy was closed forever.

Christmas was a disaster; there was no joy in the McAvoy household. Nanna did not want a tree and no decorations at all were put up. Nanna for the first time, did not bake cookies and Peeps wanted more than anything to go back to school. He tried to get more hours of work to help pass the time and save up money for wedding gifts and for tuxes; he was going to stand up in both weddings. The Older Sister was to wed in the spring and The Younger in the Fall. They both quietly went about their plans, including Nanna as much as she wanted. Dresses were ordered, invitations chosen, reception halls found. Ever so slowly the gloom began to lift. Nanna spent more time thinking about the weddings and less about her dead son. By Easter, joy had returned to Mudville. There was genuine excitement about the forthcoming weddings.

Peeps got a lot of hours during the summer; he was a valued worker and was promoted to the produce department. His boss was a cranky old guy named Gus Nitti; he was ancient, but after a few months Peeps knew more about apples, artichokes and asparagus than he ever wanted to. He began to admire his boss; he was knowledgeable and was a good teacher. He taught Peeps how to tell whether fruit was ripe and when to pull produce that was about to spoil. More importantly, he showed Peeps about the importance of customer service, which was mostly patience. He liked working at Dominick's and decided to ask for more hours after school. He would work on Tuesdays, Thursdays and Saturdays; the problem was that on the weekdays he might not get home until almost eleven. Nanna was totally against this plan and she was proved right.

He was always tired, so he hardly studied. He was behind and used every free minute to read textbooks, borrow someone else's homework and try to find a way to just get through. In Latin III, Cicero was the text and it was hard. He was in an advanced class because he had performed so well last year. Just what he needed. He tried to get out of it, but the Headmaster would have none of it. He finished his second year with a B- average; he finished the first semester of his junior year with a D+ average. The only class he did well in was Geometry. He loved it and loved the old guy that taught it with such enthusiasm. His social life was for shit; Linda and her family moved to Arlington Heights and he rarely saw her. Every four or five weeks he would skip a day at school, asking Nanna to call him in as sick. She did not like doing this, but did it anyway. His usual friends were not around as much; he was often too tired to go out on Friday nights. He spent more time with his store friends. He did not realize it, but he was in a real crisis. He did not know what to do.

Second semester he reduced his hours to just one weekday and night. But the damage had been done. His grades had improved slightly by the end of the school year. Now the pressure was college; he would never get an academic scholarship. He certainly could not afford to go away, so Loyola University looked like his best and only option. His SAT scores were just average and the Kuder Preference Test said he should be a park ranger. He had no one to talk to; Linda was not around and he was utterly and miserably on his own.

During the summer he managed to get quite a bit of work at the store. Times were good and the usual cadre of high schoolers looking for summer work did not occur. Peeps was delighted to take as many hours as he could. Further, he made a very important decision to reconnect with his buddies from the neighborhood. He had neglected them and several had told him so in no uncertain terms. Further they needed someone who looked twenty-one, and at six-two, two hundred pounds and heavy facial hair, he was just the guy. He had taken French this last year and it came in handy one night when he went to the discount store to buy. The woman, not much older than he, asked for his I.D. In a panic, he just stood there looking at her, all the while loading beer onto the counter. She asked again and he said nothing. Finally, he told her in French that he did not understand what she wanted. She persisted and he spoke French. The stand-off lasted at least five minutes. Peeps just shrugged and said that he did not understand. Exasperated, she rang up the order and Peeps left with bags of beer. Asked why it took so long, the lads roared with laughter when he told the tale.

If he could buy booze, he could buy condoms. They were sold at the pharmacy counter and you had to ask for what you wanted. Fortunately, most pharmacists were men, so the worst he would get was a smirk and asked what size he wanted. He was smart enough not to ask for XL or XXL sizes; he assumed that they did not come in a small size, an insult to any man. He settled on large and decided to go late in the evening when the store would not be busy. He spent ten minutes walking up and down the aisles of the Walgreens to make sure that no one he knew was around. The only brand he knew was Trojan so he would go the counter looking nonchalant as possible. As it turned out the pharmacist was busy and could have cared less. In two minutes he was out the door with his brown paper bag. He was all set; now he just needed a girl. For advice on that matter he went to a guy he worked with, Carl. He was not very tall and had average looks but he left the store every evening with a different girl in tow. Without bragging, he told Peeps that he got laid twice a week, with two different girls. He told Peeps that he should take some time to get to know a girl, listen to what she was interested in and not spend the night talking about himself. Then when the time is right, simply ask. Peeps would be surprised how many girls would say yes. If the answer was no, simply accept the decision like a gentleman and take her home. The next weekend he and Linda had a date; she was going to stay at her Aunt's apartment and the Aunt thankfully went to bed early. He followed Carl's advice to a tee and Peeps and Linda had a wonderful evening on the couch. God bless Auntie and God bless Linda. She confessed that she wanted to screw for months and thought it was about time he asked. He assured her he would not be so shy in the future. Give us a boy and we will give you a man.

He had his tuition money in the bank by the end of June and decided it was time to get a new car. The Corvair just was not safe; raw exhaust seeped into the car, so that even in winter Peeps had to keep the windows open when the car was running. He talked to Nanna about his plan and she readily agreed. He was too young to buy a car, so she had to put it in her name. They called The Brothers-in-Law and one of them knew a guy who knew a guy who knew a guy. For a thousand dollars they found a used Chevy and it even had air conditioning; Peeps was in seventh heaven. It had forty thousand miles on it so Peeps would have to be careful to keep it repaired. The car was larger than Nanna was used to, so the two of them went over to the huge parking lots at Montrose harbor so Nanna could practice. After a half hour Nanna drove home but had Peeps put the car in the garage.

Peeps was determined to do better his last year in school. At the end of summer, he explained to his manager that he could not work during the week this year. The manager was furious and Peeps thought he was about to get fired. He explained that he could not keep up with his work, and that senior year classes were similar to classes he would take in college. He also told him he planned on working well past high school, full time if possible while he took a course or two each semester. Mollified but not happy, they agreed to Saturdays and the short Sunday hours—the store was only open ten to two. He also got paid time and a half for Sunday work. It was a sweet deal and Peeps knew it. He also knew that the manager liked him; he showed up on time and did not screw around. He was good to customers and was willing to learn.

Senior year began with the Mass of the Holy Spirit, as always. Peeps went to communion without going to confession. He had totally rejected sex as sin long ago. He was willing to take his chances. He was much more concerned about Linda's aunt waking up in the middle of the evening and catching them in action. He gave Nanna two hundred and fifty dollars and promised her his Sunday wages to help around the house. He made over thirty dollars on Saturday and that was more than enough for a kid his age. He also told Nanna that he planned to lose some weight and would she help him build up his wardrobe. He wanted a few nice things for dates; because Nanna got a very good discount at the store, she paid and he gave her the money later. He bought shirts that actually fit for school and some ties that would match. The Jesuits stuck to the age old tradition of boys in ties, but thankfully without the blazers. Even his friends complimented him on his new look and pressed him if he was getting any from

Linda these days. He just ate his lunch, which was now down to a sandwich and some fruit. He had stopped growing and did not need all that much food.

Senior year was the hardest yet; the Jesuits clearly thought this was their last chance at intellectual torture. Latin IV was reading the Aeneid and the crazy priest that taught it knew the whole epic by heart in the original Latin. Someone would read a couple of lines from where the class left off the previous day, and Fr. Clifford would quote chapter and verse the next fifty lines. Peeps never got over this; finally one of his friends reminded him that he taught the same thing four times a day for twenty years. He could not help but memorize it. Peeps remained unconvinced; there was something about these Jesuits that just was not normal. All of them pulled rabbits out of the hat in their own ways. Senior year was also active recruitment time to get guys interested in being a Jesuit. And they were none too subtle about it, including traveling to Cincinnati for the annual retreat and to see the young Jesuits in formation. Peeps was absolutely certain that he would make a lousy Jesuit; hell, he did not even go to mass regularly.

The year sped by; he applied to Loyola University and was accepted. You would have to be absolutely stupid not to get into Loyola coming from a Jesuit high school. He was seeing less and less of Linda, which made him ache. He loved couch nights. They both agreed, however, to invite each other to their respective proms. They both knew it was a matter of convenience. By Easter every senior had virtually stopped in place, doing as little work as possible. Everyone was accepted to college and they just wanted to get the hell out. It was time to move on. Peeps actually went to three proms; a girl he knew asked him to go to the Immaculata prom and he agreed. Proms were expensive and the last one broke the bank. He borrowed fifty dollars from Nanna and managed to have a good time at all three. Peeps had a party after the Loyola prom and the guestlist was carefully controlled. Nanna allowed them to have beer but the boys had to police the event themselves. Three other guys agreed to help and told Nanna to her face that there would not be a problem. And there was not any hint of an issue.

One of his buddies from Queen of All Saints arranged to use his uncle's cottage outside of Lake Geneva; it was on a small lake for swimming and fishing. Peeps was asked to go for four days. Nanna agreed though he did not need her approval except to use the car. A big attraction was that you could buy beer at eighteen in Wisconsin. They agreed that one person each night would not have more than a beer or two. They played rock, paper, scissors to decide who would drive each night. Peeps had Thursday night and kept to his word. Even then, he almost drove another car off the road and scraped the crap out of the side of the Chevy. He was not used to narrow, winding Wisconsin roads in the pitch dark. He would have to get it repainted and doubted he could do it without telling Nanna what was going on. He might get away with it, but it would cost a bunch. The four of them realized that they had to be careful. They wanted to have a good time, not get killed on the road.

The bar scene in Lake Geneva was a blast; there were college girls everywhere. The guys spent the first evening going around and chatting up several groups of girls they thought were their own age. They really liked the five girls from the University of Wisconsin at Racine; they were lively, friendly and even though a year older, did not find that a problem. The girls invited them to their cabin for a cookout; the guys would bring wine, beer and soft drinks. The girls would cook hamburgers and hotdogs and all would swim in the lake. They set a time, got directions and the guys actually left early—partly because they were starting to run low on cash. One of the girls was from Appleton up north in Wisconsin. Her last name was Raynor. Peeps asked her if she had an elderly relative that lived in Chicago. She had, but Mrs. Raynor had died years ago. Fascinated, Peeps explained that Old Mrs. Raynor was his next door neighbor for a while and helped his parents get the house they lived in. A small world they all agreed.

Everyone got sunburned on Saturday, and Saturday night was subdued. They exchanged phone numbers and full names, promising to keep in touch. Everyone knew they would not. The guys had a blast and stayed up late at the cabin drinking and shooting the shit. Gradually they went to bed, with only Danny and Peeps still up. Danny was really drunk and he came over and sat next to Peeps, put his hand on his knee and asked if Peeps wanted a blow job. Peeps was paralyzed; he said nothing, just got up and went to bed. Cleaning up and driving home were very uncomfortable for Peeps. Danny seemed his old self; did Peeps not understand what had happened last night? Now he could not wait to get home. He drove the entire way, stopping for gas and junk food. One of the guys had a gas credit card his father had given him. They agreed to settle up later. He got off the Edens at Peterson and drove Danny to his house. He high-fived everyone and said we should do this again. Peeps just wanted to get home. He had to work the next day and had to get the car repaired. He was exhausted and very uneasy about Danny. He did not know how he was supposed to react.

CHAPTER FIVE:

Loyola University and Dominick's Finer Foods

Loyola was mostly a commuter school with huge graduate programs. The school had just started building dorms; it anticipated that students and parents would love the scenic lakefront campus and the hustle and bustle of the big city, Chicago. But as Peeps started his college career, most of the activity was centered on the student union where kids gathered en masse between classes. Peeps did not have much time to hang around and meet new kids. He knew a slew of kids from Loyola and the neighborhoods. What he lacked was introductions to girls. He had two classes in the morning and had to hustle home to change and be at work by one.

Rather than follow the advice of his counselor, Peeps checked in with some of the older students, asking what he should take. Everyone recommended the two semester class on geology, which would take care of his science requirement. He signed up for Rocks for Jocks; you had to have a frontal lobotomy to fail this class. Literally every jock and jockette in school took the class, plus assorted others like Peeps. It was a huge lecture hall, with two hundred or more eager students. Grades were based on weekly quizzes; there was no mid-term, final or even a paper to write. Copies of the quizzes were everywhere. The professor never changed them, except the order of the questions. Read the chapter each Thursday night, maybe twice if it was complicated and practice the quiz questions. The Prof. never lectured about the book content; he spent the class talking about the latest research in geology. Attendance was mandatory, so you could not escape. The lecture material was never tested. The professor was actually fascinating if you took the time to listen, and Peeps often did. He was animated, funny, insightful and deeply involved in his area of expertise.

The second class was an introduction to Catholic Theology and Tradition taught by the Reverend Jeremiah J. Flaherty, S.J., better known as the Charmer. He was middle-aged, handsome as hell, funny, likeable, and a real man's man. Father loved two things; bridge and bourbon, and not necessarily in that order. Students loved him but dreaded his class. He had taught the same material for fifteen years; even his lecture notes were yellow with age. Loyola had a tradition that all students, whether Catholic or not, had to take two semesters each of theology and philosophy—after all this was a Catholic, Jesuit university. Father had a simple grading system: A for athletes; B for boys and C for co-eds, unless they were jockettes. Every co-ed taking the class made sure that Father knew that she played soccer, basketball, softball, volleyball or swam, whether true or not.

Father Charmer was a real contradiction; like every Jesuit Peeps got to know, he had a whole other side to him. In the classroom he was pedantic and dull; outside of the classroom he was charming, outgoing and actively interested in students, whether he taught them or not. He loved to play bridge and often would go to the student union after drinks and dinner at the Jesuit residence in search of a bridge game. He was a great player and an inspired teacher; he always found students who wanted to play, especially with him. He partnered with kids that knew nothing about the game and with experienced, serious players. Normally the number of students dwindled as the evening went on—not so when Charmer was around. Everyone wanted into the game and kids just hung around to listen to the banter, watch the play and enjoy a very personable, warm man. He had an amazing ability to remember names; once told a name it was almost never forgotten. He managed to get God and religion in the conversation and always dressed in a Roman collar and was very much a Jesuit priest. He liked the young people as much as they enjoyed him. He was a great standard-bearer for the Loyola Jesuits.

Father Charmer said the twelve-thirty mass every Sunday at Madonna Della Strada, the university chapel. He packed the joint, students and faculty alike. First, his masses were quick; he knew what the crowd wanted and never disappointed. Secondly, in complete contradiction to his classroom style, he was a brilliant, talented and funny homilist. He never spoke from the altar, but took a position as close to the pews as possible. His sermons always offered a relevant message for a contemporary, college audience. He was a stage actor who knew when to be dramatic and when to pause for effect, always without notes. He would quote the day's scripture from heart as he wove his message in and through the ancient texts. Here was another Jesuit pulling rabbits out of the hat. Peeps would take Nanna once in a while, motivated to prove to his mother he was not a complete heathen.

First semester ended well; he got a B in each class. Geology went on for the second semester so he needed a second course. He decided on a philosophy course in logic, one recommended by his counselor. The course would take care of yet another requirement towards graduation. He loved the course because it reminded him of geometry. The instructor was a graduate student and actually did a pretty good job. She, too, required daily attendance and you had to sign the sheet next to your name. Peeps hated to procrastinate; he put off a writing assignment in high school and suffered from the results. He had to stay up all night to finish it, made dozens of mistakes and subsequently got a poor grade on a paper which otherwise had real merit. He worked on the first one early in the semester; the second was completed by the end of the third quarter. Nanna was there to review each draft, red pencil in hand. There seemed to be more red than typed script. Besides there was nothing else to do; it was a rotten winter and Linda had gone away for school. His social life was a blank. He received a C+ and a B on the papers; good enough thought Peeps.

Towards the end of the semester some very dark clouds were on the horizon. The geology professor missed several classes in a row. Apparently he was very sick. In his place came a gung-ho Ph. D. candidate in earth sciences. He told the class in no uncertain terms that the game was up. Yes, he would continue to have quizzes each week, with twenty questions not ten. And no, they could not find copies of his quizzes anywhere. A short paper was required and suggested one of the many topics the professor had lectured about during the semester. He would post a list. The final exam would be on the last half of the textbook and he suggested they form study groups to make up for the short time before the exam

Peeps avoided asking any of the guys to form a study group; it was a perfect way to meet some new girls and he was positive that they would take this seriously. He asked the two rather plain girls who always sat next to him and a very nice looking chick named Vicky. They all agreed immediately and met at the library to get organized and get the ball rolling. Names and telephone numbers were shared. Notes were to be typed, in outline form and in detail. All the girls looked at Peeps and asked in unison if he could type. He could indeed he assured his newest best friends. In one week to the day, each was to have four copies of a chapter ready for the group. Between the paper and outlines, Nanna's red pencil would get a workout. Part of second year English in high school was devoted to detailed instructions on how to outline. Peeps was a good student and actually liked to prepare outlines. The girls were impressed with his efforts.

The second week, Peeps called Vicky and asked her to go out. She said yes immediately. They agreed to meet at Calo's on Clark Street for pizza and beer. She was a great date, fun to listen to, engaging, animated and had a wide variety of interests. She was going to school full-time and took the geology class because she hated science and knew, like everyone else, that this was an easy way to get this required course out of the way. She told Peeps that she did not drink much, but had a beer for the sake of the evening. She ate like a stevedore; she had three quarters of a large pizza. She was not at all heavy and he wondered where she put it all. At the end of the evening, she insisted on paying half; this did not happen very often in Peeps' experience. She lived in Park Ridge and Peeps walked her to the car, getting a very nice, goodnight kiss for his trouble. He was in love again.

Grades were delivered and he got a B in logic and could not believe his eyes: an A in geology. He had no plans to take a course in the summer; he wanted out of school for a while. Besides he had other issues, Vicky being high on the priority list. He was short of cash and Nanna announced that they had problems; she needed a new air conditioner and a new refrigerator. There was no market for used appliances; if you buy used, you really take a huge risk she explained. Peeps put his school money into the house and had to work hard to make tuition money for next year. As to Vicky, he planned to spend every second he could with her. They met the next weekend for a movie at the Pickwick in Park Ridge and he walked her home—just a few blocks from the theater. Vicky was very quiet this night and he asked if she was ok. She said yes. They got to her house to settle down on the front porch for some serious necking and petting when the porch light went on. Without turning around, both waved to her mother. Peeps, having only met her once, was certain that she did not like him. Her daughter could do better. They started to kiss and Vicky stopped short, telling Peeps that she had something very important to say. His stomach muscles went tight; he was sure she was going to dump him. She did not want to lead him on; she had decided to go into the convent, following her aunt who was a Sister of Mercy. She would leave for the novitiate in late July, somewhere in Iowa.

He was stunned and had no words, so he sat and listened for nearly an hour. The light flicked on and off several times and Vicky finally got up and told her mother she would sit on the porch with Peeps for as long as she wanted; she demanded she go to bed and stop the childish games. The light went off and so did Peeps; he said goodnight, gave her a kiss and asked if they could go out one more time before she left. She said that was not a good idea; she had to make a break and this was the time. By the time he got home and parked the car, he found Nanna was still up. She knew Peeps really liked this Vicky person and looked forward to meeting her. After Peeps told her the Vicky story, Nanna sat for a moment and then burst out laughing. She hugged him and apologized for her laughter. Leaving for bed, she looked at her crestfallen son and explained that it was the McAvoy luck. Peeps stayed up with a bunch of beer and the television as his only consolation. Nanna found him, the early news on when she came down to go to work.

Two weeks later and still smarting about Vicky, the manager called Peeps into his office to tell him that he was being promoted to assistant produce manager. There were hints that when Gus retired, Peeps would take over. The pay raise was nearly seventy dollars a month. He was management now and told him he had to act like it. He also was told that he and Gus would go to Northbrook for training on the company's new computer based order processing system. Many of Peeps' friends had computers and he spent time on theirs. He did not have the money and the need for one, but maybe the time had come to get more experience and buy a basic unit. Peeps was thrilled with the three day training program; Gus was terrified. He had to do well; he would work like a fool to make sure he mastered the system. Computers were going to be everywhere shortly and Peeps could not afford to be left behind.

Not surprisingly Gus floundered, and badly. He was by far the oldest person in the room and had been using the same manual ordering system for thirty years. After the first morning, and dozens of questions from Gus later, the trainers decided to work with him alone, a tutorial as it were. The other nine made good progress and gained confidence by the day. For three months, produce managers would use both the manual and computer-based system. After that the manual system would be dropped. The following Monday, he came in early only to find out that Gus had not even started his order. Sure he had the manual part finished, but he did not even know how to log on and create a password. The order was supposed to be posted by eleven o'clock; Peeps took over, made a few mistakes and managed to complete everything by mid-afternoon. Peeps was sure that their store would not be the only one to be late. He was wrong and there was hell to pay. Instead of being grateful, Gus blamed the whole mess on Peeps. He was furious and told the store manager the real story—right in front of Gus. The manager asked Gus to log on and review his order. Of course he could not do so.

In revenge, Gus made Peeps' life miserable all week; he took it without a word. Peeps came in at his usual time of one o'clock on Monday. Gus wanted to play hard ball, he would return the favor. Again there was hell to pay; the manager was getting heaps of shit from his boss and he planned to let it all slide downhill. In a rage, he went to the produce department; only Gus was there as Peeps did not report until later. He demanded to know why only the manual order was finished; Gus tried to say it was Peeps' responsibility to manage the computer. It did not float; the store manager asked how often Peeps completed the inventory order under the old system. Gus had to admit never. It was the manager's job. Gus had one week to master the system or he would be demoted. When Peeps came in, he and the store manager had a very strained conversation. He admired Peeps for playing tough; he had balls. He also knew that Peeps could walk out tomorrow and get a job at another Dominick's store and at any Jewel in the city.

A quiet peace settled in; fresh produce, flowers and small gifts were increasingly an important part of the store. With each remodel, Peeps' produce department was enlarged with more employees. That is when Gina Corso came into his life. She moved from cashier to produce, part-time in the evenings. It was Peeps' job to train her and he was more than happy to do so. He figured out that she was a year ahead of him in school; she was also working almost full time and taking two or three courses at Northeastern State University on the northwest side. She wanted to take her core classes at Northeastern which was cheap and fairly basic in terms of academics. Her goal was to transfer eventually to Loyola for nursing school. Peeps was impressed; she had her shit together. Peeps, by contrast, did know what he was going to do beyond next Thursday.

Part of the peace was that Peeps would come in early on Mondays to get the produce order into the system. After a month or so, he found that he could load the data in about forty-five minutes. Gus said nothing, never thanked him. After one particularly annoying Monday, he informed Gus in no uncertain terms that this was his last time doing this. He politely explained to the store manager that he should not have to come in on his time, without pay, to do the manager's job, who made hundreds more a month that he did. The store manager said nothing; he was right of course, and on Tuesday, Gus retired and on Wednesday, Peeps was promoted to produce manager, with a two hundred and fifty dollar a month increase in pay. One day a week, he was to report to company headquarters for the next four weeks for training. He was to wear a suit and tie and had to complete the program successfully to stay on as manager.

Most of the people at the training sessions were older than Peeps; there was one woman in the group. And she was the best; she had a two year degree from a junior college in business and had a strong management background. The curriculum included hiring and firing, employee discipline and reviews, history of Dominick's and its business philosophy. A great deal of the time was spent on cost containment, inventory management, and profitability. Each department in each store was a profit center and the company looked at monthly sales and profitability very carefully. Bonuses and raises were based on performance, with only a small part linked to time on the job. Peeps had homework each week and quizzes on everything from labor law to basic accounting. He never worked harder in his life; the assistant store managers, ten years his senior, assured him he would do fine as long as he did his work. He brought the study materials to the store and asked other managers for their help when needed. Everyone had been through the same sausage machine and were willing to help.

Peeps was in love with Gina; he asked her out and they had a blast. He did explain that he could not socialize frequently until his management training was finished. She understood completely and even volunteered to quiz him before each Tuesday. It was a huge help and he thanked her profusely.

No grades or ranking were given for company training; it was simply pass or fail. Thanks to the woman manager, who was in his study group, he could read an income statement, knew the difference between a debit and a credit and could read and understand T accounts. He mastered the weekly financial statements each manager received from corporate and worked against these to manage his department. The store manager congratulated him and told Peeps on the sly that the trainers were impressed with his work and study habits. He now started to think about making retailing his career path. Now he had time to concentrate on Gina; they went out again and Peeps asked her to come to his house; he had wine and beer in the basement refrigerator, a stereo and a very comfortable couch. And they would have privacy. They came into the house through the basement door, after all it was after ten and they did not want to wake Nanna. Peeps served some rose with crackers and cheese and excused himself while he took a shower. He was nervous, eager and aroused; he wanted to go slow and not make a fool of himself. He had hardly washed his hair, when the door opened and the lovely, naked Gina piled into the small shower. Between kissing, they both made sure that they washed the other important parts, several times to make sure. They made love twice that night and Peeps was fairly certain that Gina could have gone for round three. He was exhausted.

Getting together once or twice a week became their habit. On the weekends, they would go out for dinner or a show. Gina never stayed the night. She did not want to be embarrassed in front of Nanna. Besides she lived at home and did not want to explain what was going on to her parents. She met Nanna for the first time when she volunteered to make Sunday dinner for the three of them. She chose a simple pasta, with an Italian salad and cannoli for dessert. They had a great time. After a bit, Nanna told the kids she was going to bed early just in case they wanted to listen to music downstairs. With a twinkle in her eye, she kissed both goodnight and went off to bed. She had a good amount of red wine, nearly a full bottle she thought. She had to be a bit more careful in the future. She liked to drink, like everyone else in the family.

Two weeks later, as Gina and Peeps were coming through the basement door, Nanna opened the first floor door and frantically asked them to come upstairs. She apologized for ruining their evening, but she received a registered letter in the mail that had her so upset, she panicked and started to scream. The envelope was addressed to the estate of Randy McAvoy from a law firm in Washington D.C.; in essence the letter demanded two hundred and fifty thousand dollars as compensation for the untimely death of one Gloria Glintz. If some reasonable accommodations were not made a civil lawsuit would be filed in Federal Court in Washington. The estate had ten days to respond. Gina had no idea what was going on, so Peeps sat her down, pulled out a bottle of Italian red and the Jameson's; mother and son had two fingers without ice, as Peeps explained in brief the history of his brother and the way he went off to college.

After they reassured themselves that they could not possibly be responsible, Nanna reminded Peeps that her Will was on the third shelf of the pantry, next to the can of baked beans which had been there for at least ten years. She said nothing about the details of her Will except that Randy was not part of her estate. Randy was eighteen when he left home and there was nothing of his in the house. Peeps had thrown away a few items of clothes, sports trophies and his collection of well-thumbed Playboy magazines the day after his dramatic parting. He wanted nothing to remind him of his brother. Strangely, Peeps thought, Gina asked about his mail. Nanna thought a bit and said she has never seen anything in his name came to the house except the Georgetown letter advising Randy of his loss of scholarship. In fact, Nanna could not remember any mail in the months before his leaving.

Gina made the point that they ought to try to prove he had changed his address before actually leaving; that might help to show that Randy was an adult living on his own, never mind that there was no money or assets. Everything he had of value went to Washington in those three suitcases. Perhaps, she reasoned that no claim could be made on Nanna, Peeps, the house and their financial assets. Before Gina left, they made a short list of things to do. The post office was one; Nanna would call Detective Small once again to ask if he would help identify this Gloria Glintz. Peeps would call The Sisters for a council of war on these people from Washington. They needed a lawyer, one they could afford. Gina suggested calling the State's Attorney's office to file a fraud complaint and to check on this law firm in D.C. Peeps walked Gina to her car and kissed her goodnight. When he got back he added a finger of whiskey and an ice cube to their drinks, and Nanna and her boy sat at the table for a half hour preoccupied with their own thoughts. Neither had to work early in the morning, so they had time to catch up on sleep and get a good night's rest. Neither slept a wink; Nanna had Peeps drive her to the Rogers Park post office to begin the process of finding the proverbial needle in a haystack—a change of address card filed by Randy McAvoy sometime in the last year.

Even though she was there when the post office opened, Nanna somehow found herself fifth in line. It was slow going; she reached the clerk after twenty minutes. She explained what she wanted and was simply told no; Nanna tried again, a bit frustrated and a tad louder. What she wanted was impossible. She started again a third time explaining it was a matter of hundreds of thousands of dollars. The clerk would not budge; others in line were mumbling their complaints. At the fourth round, she was turned over to a supervisor who affirmed the clerk: No, the cards were post office property. Their argument got heated and finally the manager, a fellow named Jackson, came out. Mr. Jackson rarely spoke to customers and did everything in his power to never leave his office. He worked for the Postal Service for over thirty-five years and was promoted regularly for doing absolutely the minimum. This crazy woman was disrupting his schedule; he had just started the sports section and did not see any reason to spend his precious time with a very erratic woman shouting about hundreds of thousands of dollars.

He said no and it was time for her to leave. Nanna got louder and into his physical space, backing him into a corner. She talked to him like a dog who had just soiled the living room rug. Jackson explained that he had no one to look through a year of records; Nanna had him. She would do it. No, she could not take the card; she had money for the copy machine. He had to call his superior; she would not let him get away, informing him he had the authority. His coffee was cold by now and his danish was getting stale. He wanted to read the story in the paper about the new, young Bulls' player. Nanna put her arms in front of her chest and just stared him down. Jackson started to sweat even though the air conditioning was on high. He blinked and Nanna knew she had him. They agreed she would come in tomorrow, Nanna's day off, and she would work until she found the change of address card. Victorious, she thanked Jackson for being a warm, understanding and caring civil servant. Jackson smiled, ran to his office and made another pot of coffee, pissed that he gave into that woman. Maybe she would not show up as agreed. When she came in the next day, she found that the cards, sorted by month and in alpha order, were on a small table in a tiny cubicle. She found the card in fifteen minutes, copied it and left in triumph. Randy had filed a change of address just after high school graduation to a post office box in Washington. No wonder no one ever saw any mail for him.

Peeps took two hours off from work, explaining to the assistant store manager that he had a family crisis. There was no issue as he rarely took time off. He asked Gina to cover for him until closing and raced to Park Ridge to meet the Sisters. The Starbucks was empty when he arrived, except for The Sisters. They spent the first ten minutes cursing Randy and calling him every name they could think of. The Older Sister would have her husband check out the law firm in D.C. and she would call the State's Attorney's office and ask how to go about filing a formal complaint. The Younger Sister would work on an attorney; they knew several from Church and she was pretty sure she could get help for next to nothing. She and the Brother-in-Law had done several favors in a time of crisis and it was *quid pro quo* time. Peeps reported on Nanna the tiger's success at the post office. They had ample proof that Randy was not a part of the family and that the family had not supported him once he left for college.

The next on the list was Detective Small and Gloria Glintz. Peeps volunteered so that Nanna would not have to relive the whole horrible mess. On his day off, Peeps spent the day on the phone; he called three times before finding Small in the office. The Detective remembered the case and Nanna very well. After explaining about the letter and the demand for a money settlement or a civil trial, Peeps told the detective that there was no estate and as Randy was over eighteen, was on his own, that they saw no realistic claim. Small cautioned him to be careful and he would, as a favor to Nanna, see what he could find out about old Gloria. The neighbor-lawyer, John, gladly agreed to help on the case; so far so good. He spoke directly to the woman named on the letter and explained that there was no estate, no assets of any kind and that Mr. McAvoy was buried in a Potter's field in Maryland. The response was that Randy's family would have to pay for Gloria's untimely death. There was ample proof that he caused Gloria's death by giving her drugs.

Detective Small came through big time. Gloria Glintz was known by the Washington police. She had been arrested multiple times for selling drugs and for prostitution. She had a file an inch thick, even if it was on a computer screen. She, too, was found dead from an overdose the same night Randy died, right next to him. She was thirty-six years of age and had been in and out of rehab, paid for by her wealthy parents. Her body was claimed and cremated by the family, so there was no possibility of examining the remains, beyond the coroner's reports. Those reports confirmed a habitual drug user who had died of an overdose. The Glintz lawyer made it perfectly clear that the family wanted justice for their daughter; someone had to pay for her death. The motivation for the demand and the civil lawsuit could now be challenged for what it was — a grieving family wanting revenge from anyone.

Letters and faxes went back and forth between the lawyers. They were increasingly acrimonious and threatening. Two weeks later the family received notice that a civil lawsuit had been filed in federal court in Washington. At this point The Sisters did not want to take advantage of their lawyer friend and together wrote a check for five hundred dollars for his work thus far. He was very appreciative, as it was painfully clear that this matter was not going to be resolved easily. For his part, John, was getting into the fight; it was a real chance to engage as a lawyer in a serious matter. He had his balls in a lather and wanted to beat this woman. The more he got worked up, the more pissed he was— especially the absolute abuse of the court system to rob a family of a huge sum of money. In short order, the McAvoys and their lawyer scored a big victory. The federal court rejected the lawsuit, explaining in blunt terms that the suit had been filed in the wrong court; further they found little merit to the claims made by the plaintiff. There was joy in Mudville that night.

John was not finished; he met with the family in Park Ridge at The Younger Sister's house and outlined a new plan. They would counter-sue the Glintzs in a district court asking for one million dollars in damages and loss of affection. John could not believe that the other lawyer had filed with the wrong court; a first year law student would know better. But it gave them time to get a jump ahead. With the help from a friend from law school who lived in Maryland, John prepared the suit with a demand for damages. He also returned the check given to him for services. Instead he produced a contract that allowed John to keep twenty-five percent of any proceeds from the lawsuit. From now on, he would work on a contingency basis, including covering any expenses such as travel and paralegal help.

From this point forward, the family would only think of Randy as a loved and devoted son and brother. They had no reason to talk about his hateful exit from the house or about his change of address filing. They would admit that he was difficult and self-absorbed. They would each be interviewed under oath and they were to tell the truth. He had no history of drug abuse; he was brilliant and popular with his friends; he had a promising career, beginning with his Georgetown scholarship. Peeps was assigned the task of getting written testimonials from friends and faculty at Loyola Academy. Why did they throw his trophies away? They were a painful reminder of who this young man was—no lie there. John prepped them further and they all readily agreed to John's plan. If they did get money damages, it would truly be for pain and suffering.

Peeps would love to have been a fly on John's office wall when opposing counsel called. She was beyond livid. John made it clear that both people had died in a pile of trash, right next to each other. Only one of them was a known junkie and pusher. Randy had no drug history and an impeccable personal record. He never got a traffic ticket. As the woman raged, John sat back, listened, said little and smiled to himself. He ended the conversation, as she had run out of swear words, with the suggestion that the Glintz family could always settle rather than be humiliated in front of their Georgetown friends.

Months went by with no communication between the parties. John explained that the suit would be reviewed for its merits, and if it met legal precedent, would be placed on the docket. The good news was no counter suit was filed. John thought this was very promising.

The McAvoys went about their business as best they could; the longer the process went on the less frightening it seemed. They thought John brilliant and very tough; he was a great find and The Second Sister got much praise and thanks for finding him. Peeps' work had been suffering a bit, so he renewed his energy to get back into the groove. His ordering improved and his choice for the woman to run the floral section was brilliant. They did not get along very well, so they tried to stay out of each other's way. After six months, he was able to persuade the boss to give her a substantial raise. She almost made what an assistant manager would make, but without the title. At the end of the year, he received an award from Dominick's and a cash bonus of five hundred dollars.

He and Gina went out to celebrate and ended the evening very satisfactorily on the couch, as was their custom.

Gina had bought a new wrinkle to their love making; she liked to sit naked and read dirty poems. She began with Canto One from a self-described rakish poem, Don Juan, by Lord Byron. She would read random parts of various cantos, in a soft, velvety voice. She had other poems, of course, a whole book of them. This was not a book you would check out from Loyola U's library. Peeps would just close his eyes and listen; at times he understood subtle poetry; the completely crude ones brought a smile to his face. After fifteen or twenty minutes of poetry reading he was so aroused he could scream. Their lovemaking was fierce after each reading. Gina was always fun and interesting, talking about classes she was taking, people she met at school and, of course, her family. She was very concerned about the pending lawsuit and they talked about it often, even though nothing was happening. They never left the store at the same time and never in the same car. Peeps was not sure how management would react if it found out about their relationship. At the store, it was strictly business. They were not sure if they were fooling anyone, but kept up the charade anyway.

One Thursday Gina left Peeps a note that she wanted to go out for a drink instead of the basement couch. Peeps could hardly complain; they blessed the couch faithfully twice a week. They went over to Western Avenue to a new place called Gene's for drinks and sandwiches. Gina was very serious tonight; she wanted to know why Peeps had not signed up for a second semester class. She understood why he took the Fall semester off, but why was he not going to school as planned. Peeps hemmed and hawed and admitted that he just had lost interest. He also explained that he was scheduled for a second corporate training session and thought that these met his goals better than general studies at Loyola. Gina worked hard to change his mind. She felt he had no plan; he countered that he was the youngest manager in the district and thought he had a real future in retail. The evening ended badly for both of them. Suddenly, Peeps thought he had woman problems, but was not sure.

Just as suddenly, John received notice from the court that it had accepted the lawsuit and put in on the docket for early May. John told everyone to be prepared; depositions would be taken, paperwork would pile in and evidence gathered. Of extreme importance was the police blotter and the number of times Gloria Glintz was arrested and convicted for selling drugs and her family's involvement in her life. She was their dependent, despite her age. John would obtain bank records of money transferred to Gloria, the payment for rehab and other evidence of their responsibility for their daughter. John felt these links would be important for the case. There was a three week hiatus before the family heard anything more about their case. Mrs. Glintz wanted out of this lawsuit and to close for good her daughter's life; she wanted to settle. Her husband was adamant not to settle but to take it to court. The couple finally agreed that they would settle for fifty thousand dollars. John rejected the offer and countered with two hundred thousand. They settled on one fifty and once the paperwork was completed, John received a cashier's check, took his fees and sent each family member one fourth of the remaining money. Mother and children were ecstatic about the settlement. Upon receipt of the funds, the lawsuit was withdrawn.

By spring Peeps and Gina rarely went out anymore. Peeps knew it was over, Gina reminded Peeps that she was going to University of Illinois in the fall to start her nursing program. She had changed her mind about Loyola; it was too expensive. Peeps had Nanna, The Sisters, and his friends but he was already feeling lonely.

CHAPTER SIX:
Nanna Redux

Even though she went by the name of Nanna, she did not feel like a grandmother. She rarely saw her daughters and grandkids. Everyone was always busy; the women made excuses. Except for the holidays, their visits were infrequent. This was a huge disappointment. She woke up one morning and could not recognize the face in the mirror. Middle-age had come and was on its way out. While normally an optimistic person by nature, the last twenty years had made her introspective and concerned about her children, herself and her life. The old friends at the store had mostly retired, her sisters had long ago moved out of state and she found that her only real friends were four or five women who lived on Hood St. She was lonely and increasingly dependent on Peeps for moral support and financial assistance.

After years of success at the department store, she was concerned about her job. She had no pension plan; she could not afford to retire at age sixty-two—the earliest she could apply for her own social security. She would receive minimal benefits; she had to hold out until sixty-five. What worried her the most was that the store might close. Neighborhood department stores were increasingly under pressure from suburban malls. It was no secret at work that the new president, the founder's son, was very concerned about sales and profits. She often talked to Peeps about how backward the inventory and buying systems were. There was not a computer in the place; they could not find out what they were selling at the register like modern stores did. Women's dresses and her own department had only one part-time person to cover both departments. Younger women from the neighborhood did not shop at the store.

With her paycheck was a note from Allen, the owner, asking department managers to come one hour early on Monday. Nanna's stomach was in knots the entire weekend. Allen began by explaining the financial facts of life; the store was losing money and the family was not sure how long they could hang on without some drastic changes. He was open to ideas. Nanna took a bold step and asked which departments made money: the men's store, which sold classic quality goods; the children's department, and of all things, the fabric and notions department in the basement. The volume was not huge but the margins were; further they stocked goods that appealed to several ethnic groups. The buyer did a great job. Nanna and others suggested that they expand the children's department, stocking quality goods with high margins. Allen announced that the shoe store would close and that space would allow for expansion for children's wares. They would combine all women's goods under one manager. It was not Nanna; she was crestfallen and scared. Instead, she would take over the expanded kid's area. She almost fainted. They planned a huge rummage sale, and would advertise like crazy. If necessary, they would sell at cost to get rid of as much inventory as possible. They would then announce the new Winsberg's. A friend of Allen's would take over space in the women's area and bring in a free-standing jewelry store.

While the store was closed for two weeks for remodeling, Nanna spent days downtown to find out what the State Street stores were selling. She made copious notes, checked prices and asked sales people about the best brands to stock. They were surprisingly helpful. Nanna spent some time with her neighbors and asked about young families moving into the neighborhood. Once the store reopened, Nanna met with Allen to talk about what she had learned and her first major buy for the Fall and winter season. Allen cut the buy by ten percent and told her to go ahead. She and her two assistants worked like peasants to make the area bright, clean, fresh and inviting. After a week, the difference was amazing.

With the employment crisis abated for the moment, Nanna became an amateur real estate guru. The house next-door had sold again to a couple who owned a True Value franchise. They paid over two-hundred and ninety thousand dollars for the house. That did not include the mob of workmen that descended on the house like locusts to repair, paint, remodel and land-scape. They spent money like water. Connie and Larry Havisham were busy people, without children. Nanna made it a point to bake and invite herself and Peeps over one Sunday afternoon. To everyone's delight, the families got along famously, the common ground was that all of them were invested heavily into retail. Nanna asked why they chose St. Gertude and Edgewater Glen for a home. The answer was simple: great houses, cheaply priced in a stable neigh-borhood. Larry reported that there was a lot of interest in the area. Prices were half of Lakeview and a quarter of the price for a home in Lincoln Park. Every-one wanted to live by the lake.

Nanna talked of nothing else for the entire week; Peeps watched nervously as she began plans for improving their house. She was fascinated by gardening, which meant that Peeps was now fascinated with gardening. She set her sights on redoing the inside and outside of the house, room by room and area by area. She now set Peeps sights on home remodeling. Time for chasing women and drinking at the Bubble were in serious jeopardy. Peeps did his very best to slack off; he avoided anything that remotely looked like gardening and home improvement. But Nanna was way ahead of him. She pulled out her Will, the one sitting next to the twenty-year-old can of baked beans, and placed it on the table right in front of his nose. She dropped the bomb that she was leaving the house to him alone; The Sisters were well established and did not need the money. She told him straight out that when she died and if the house was sold, he would have no place to go. Peeps was overwhelmed; the unopened will went back on the pantry shelf, next to the can of baked beans.

A dynamo in action, Nanna invited six of the ladies on the street for lemon-ade and cookies on the front porch. A bottle of gin (for gin bucks) was conve-niently within arm's reach should further refreshment be required. Half-way through the gin, Nanna stomped her foot and clapped loudly to get everyone's attention, not an easy task. She finally got them to stop the gossip and listen for a few minutes. Nanna talked about her new neighbors and what they had said about the future of the neighborhood. She told them that their houses were worth much more than what they had been selling for. She told of her plans to remodel and landscaping the front and side yards. She also told about the woman on Norwood, a real estate agent, who had been saying that houses were selling too cheaply—this same mantra for years. Everyone nodded knowingly, except for Sally who said no one would get the money they were putting into the house when it came time to sell. Sally was adamant and Nanna increasingly loud and argumentative. This set off a lively discussion for the next two hours. For his part, Peeps went to the store for another bottle of Tanqueray.

Peeps and Nanna went to work. Peeps discovered skills he did not know he had. When he had a problem, he would talk to Larry who was very knowledgeable about plumbing, kitchen repair, painting, carpentry and a host of domestic skills. For his part, Peeps went out of his way to buy everything he could at Larry's store, even though it was not close; he became one of Larry's best customers. Once the garden was established, it was time to repaint. Fortunately, the stucco was in great condition, especially for a ninety year old house. Minor cracks were carefully repaired and the entire house was power washed to get rid of loose dirt and debris. Nanna put on her grubbies and joined the fun; Peeps went up on the ladder to paint the top two thirds and Nanna followed, roller in hand to work the bottom third. It took three weekends to complete the house, a gleaming medium green with white trim.

The renovators decided on a white picket fence for the front and side. They broke tradition and put a six foot solid fence with a locked gate to block the alley. This brought Sally to the house with the intent to do damage. She decried this kind of fence; it blocked neighbors from seeing each other and just did not fit into the neighborhood. She was loud and obnoxious and finally Peeps told her to shut her mouth and go home. Sally stomped out threatening to have the entire neighborhood against them. Within a month, Peeps helped two neighbors build similar fences. Nanna was also asked if the house was for sale at least three times. The painting was infectious; men and teenage boys worked the fall weekends painting their houses. Half the Mates at the Bubble would not talk to him for a month, blaming him for starting this house painting business.

How could Peeps explain to them that he was a mama's boy and how could he, Peeps, refuse his mama. Like a skin rash, it would all pass, or so reasoned Peeps.

Nanna's next reclamation project was Peeps himself. She made a wonderful steak dinner and afterward while cleaning up broached the subject of how he lived, his clothing, his social life and everything else she could think of. First, she started with the mandatory temperance lecture, pointing out that in recent months he had spent much less time and money at the Bubble because of the work on the house; he looked great. She complimented him on losing fifteen pounds; but he needed new clothes desperately. They agreed to go to Winsberg's for some better clothes and Sears for work clothes. Five hundred dollars lighter, Peeps was pleased as hell. Now he just needed a woman. Nanna bought this delicate subject up; while she was impressed that he had taken up reading with a passion, he was much too young and good-looking to spend his time drinking martinis and reading the current bestsellers. Her suggestion was to get a dog and spend the evenings walking the dog throughout the neighborhood and especially along the lake. Girls loved single guys with a dog.

Marcus the Dog came into their lives two weeks later. Sadly, Nanna found out that a lady from church was very sick and going to hospice. She was looking for a nice home for her dog. Nanna took the initiative, without telling Peeps, and he came home from work to find a dog knee high, friendly as could be and mercifully house broken. The only problem was that Marcus was a digger and Nanna and Marcus had multiple face to snout retraining sessions until she was satisfied that her garden was safe. At first Peeps felt a bit foolish walking a little dog around the hood. Armed with plastic baggies, he would even take the dog into the Bubble; the owner Larry was not thrilled but did not say much. After all Peeps had probably paid his mortgage for the last twenty years. What could he say?

Marcus the wonder dog and Peeps became a neighborhood fixture; he met people, mostly other dog owners, whom he never knew existed. Nanna was right; the dog was a chick magnet. Unfortunately, many of the chicks were hens, twice his age. One small success was Lynn, whom he had met several times. Their dogs did not get along, but they always had a nice chat. Peeps judged her to be four or five years younger than him, a bit on the chunky side, but overall a very pleasant woman. After several meetings, Peeps would walk her part of the way home. He knew she lived on Hollywood, in one of the four-plus-ones that filled the street. She never allowed him to walk her to her apartment; after all this was a complete stranger, no matter how nice he was. She disappeared just as quickly as she appeared, however. He even mentioned her to Nanna.

Months later Lynn was walking her dog and met Peeps near Broadway. She was obviously on her way home. She wanted to talk in the worst way, Peeps thought. So she stayed and bent his ear for half an hour. She had troubles: ex-husband troubles, money troubles, kid problems—she had three under ten—and family troubles. Peeps was caught off-guard completely and showed it. He was embarrassed that he was so transparent; he could not wait to get away. He just was not equipped to deal with layers of financial and emotional complexity. All of his relationships with women had been simple, easy going, women with strong personalities who could manage their lives. He had never encountered such a messy emotional tangle. As he started to back away, Lynn invited him home. Her neighbor was watching the kids for an hour and they would all be in bed by the time they got home. Lynn reeked of a woman who wanted loving; Peeps had not been in bed with a woman for two years. He needed sex as much as she did. But he also realized that this was a trap of sorts. Which would win, his dick or his brain? He excused himself and went home. Boy, was he tempted. He told his Mates at the Bubble about this encounter the next night; one said he should fuck her and forget her. He was divorced twice and lived at the Bubble. The other two were married, and assured him in no uncertain terms that he did the right thing. There are plenty of ladies who had their shit together; why invite trouble. Easy for them to say; just where were these together ladies, Peeps wondered.

Nanna gave her handy-andy two months reprieve from home remodeling as she did not want the house a mess for the holidays. They also had spent all of their renovation money on new windows for the front and back of the house. They would buy the others next fall. Peeps paid most of the cost. Besides, Nanna was preoccupied with the store and the holiday selling season. She convinced Allen to have a huge sale of spring and summer clothes in early October. They were willing to break even if necessary to clear out inventory and produce needed cash. The prices were so good there was barely a sock left for sale. They vowed to repeat this rummage sale every year. They did not have the space or the cash to hold goods for the next season.

To everyone's relief, the store had a banner holiday selling season, despite the fact that the economy was not the best. Managers even received a small bonus and profuse thanks from Allen for all the hard work. Because it was a very cold winter, Nanna decided to put off a sale of fall and winter clothes. January and February, typically very slow retail months, were better than expected. Winsberg's had a decent March sale and inventory began to pour in for the spring and summer. The next year followed like the previous year; sales were up and the new Winsberg's was holding its own. Allen leased another part of the store to a dry cleaner. The cleaners brought a lot of traffic into the store. Plus they paid rent. Then the bombshell.

Allen announced to the managers that he was opening two new stores, a men's store in Old Town called the Kingston Shop and Kids Klothes in Lincoln Park. Nanna was to buy for both locations and manage the new store, located on Clark and Diversey. The 1200 square foot store would have two check outs and would be compact and filled with inventory. The location was great; the neighborhood wealthy, and foot traffic on the street phenomenal. Nanna begged, really nagged, Allen for a computerized inventory and integrated register system plus the training to use the program correctly. Allen relented and Nanna went to computer school at age sixty two. She was excited and panicked at the same time. She thought Peeps might be able to help her; as it turned out, it was the same software used by Dominick's, just on a smaller scale. She worked with a retail designer to set the store up to enhance sales—including huge, colorful graphics and modern, functional displays. A part-time window dresser came in each month to change out the display. Now when she looked into the mirror in the mornings she recognized a new, energized woman.

The new store created problems for Nanna that she never contemplated. Every morning she had to get up forty-five minutes earlier in order to catch the Broadway bus, which ran part of the way on Clark Street, and dropped her in front of the store. She had never commuted to work before and she found it exhausting. By the time she got home, she ached and was so tired she often would make a sandwich for dinner if Peeps was not around. She always got a seat going to work, rarely found one coming home unless someone got up and gave up his seat. The one bright spot, besides good sales, was Wally Bedford, who managed the Kingston Shop. She got to know him through work and they became friends, occasionally having a quiet dinner at Calo or one of the neighborhood restaurants. Two or three times a week he would drive her to work or pick her up. At times he would stop at the house and have a drink. Peeps had a huge grin on his face: Nanna had a boyfriend. She was doing better than he was.

Although he was slightly younger and divorced, Nanna was delighted to have a man in her life after all these years. She had no expectations of marriage, and, in fact, did not want to take this beyond a social friendship—until the Saturday night Wally invited her to his apartment for dinner and whatever. She never had a better time in her life and was absolutely radiant when she looked into the mirror. The whatever was wonderful. She thought she would do this more often. She did not stay the night, but took a cab home at a somewhat respectable hour. Peeps was still out with friends so there was no awkward meeting in the hallway. There was a lot to be said for whatever. Good for a girl of any age, she mused.

Round three of work chaos emerged when Allen told his managers he was closing Winsberg's for good. He had an offer from an auto parts company who would tear down the multi-storied portion of the building for a parking lot and use the newer section for the store. He did not discuss particulars, but everyone was dying to know what he got for the building. The sad part was that a neighborhood institution would die an ignominious death and thirty jobs lost. His plan was to concentrate on the two smaller stores, possibly additional outlets for one or both in the future. Nanna survived the massive lay off but felt terrible about the others, many of whom she had known for years. She was delighted but at the same time she felt terribly guilty. Two people made comments to her face as to why she was still working and they were not. She got on the Clark Street bus and got the hell out of there. She would not attend any event about the closing. She did not have the emotional capital to deal with radical change.

Nanna had just turned sixty-three and had two more years of work to reach age sixty-five, the magic age for much better Social Security income. She would need every penny of it. Her personal crusade, besides finding a woman for Peeps, was to work her ass off to make sure the store lasted a few more years. She had already noticed a small drop off in sales because the economy has turned sour once again. She and her customers knew they could find cheaper clothes for kids at the box stores and she was determined to fight like hell to compete. After consulting Allen, her first task was to cancel some orders for inventory for the following season. She had to keep expenses down. She also could not afford to be sick, even though her knees were starting to bother her. If she were out of the picture for a month, she would not have a job when she came back. Simple as that.

Now to Peeps. She encouraged Peeps to take Marcus the wonder dog to places other than around the immediate neighborhood. Take a walk in the evening along Clark Street in Andersonville; it was lively with bars and restaurants and there were always people on the street. For his part, he hated discussing his lack of women friends with his mother. Imagine the disgrace and embarrassment with his Mates at the Bubble if it ever came out that a grown man was talking dates and sex with his mother. What the hell, he thought; Marcus and Peeps would venture out and walk Clark Street to see what was what. Marcus was a huge success; he met three women, lovelies all, and Peeps chatted them up until husbands or boyfriends showed up, one of whom was the size of a mini-van. But he did have two successful encounters, both gay guys who wanted to know if he was up for a drink. Hmm. Marcus, maybe you are not the wonder dog after all. Peeps wondered if it was too late to join the Jesuits.

Next Nanna suggested focusing on the store. After all, he had met several wonderful girls there in the past. Peeps explained to Nanna that he was a manager and could not hit on the employees; he would lose his job. But, he thought, customers were fair game. Not to be too obvious, he started slowly, paying attention to women about his age. He was particularly good, as he was taught, at helping customers. And he remembered what his co-worker Carl advised years ago. It seemed to Peeps good advice and still a way to act with women. First, Peeps ditched his work clothes; he wore khakis instead of jeans. Next he bought long-sleeved white cotton shirts. Next came a collection of ties, most of which he bought in better resale shops, making sure they were silk and in style. He worked at losing ten pounds and had his hair cut more frequently and even covered some emerging gray hair with an over-the-counter gel. He was ready to meet the women of Dominick's, whatever that would bring.

Peeps spent less and less time on the floor arranging avocados, asparagus and apples, even though Nanna had become a whiz at getting stains out of shirts—she had at least ten bottles of stuff to handle any emergency Peeps brought home. More than half the day was spent on the computer, ordering, looking at resumes, and finalizing reports to management about department performance. His new look was noticed by the store manager, Terry, who ironically had once been a Jesuit. Terry was as Irish as Paddy's pig and they got along famously. One fine day, as they say, Peeps struck up a conversation with Jeannie, a customer about his age, give or take. She came in a few days later and asked his advice about casaba melons. Melons, however interpreted, were Peeps' specialty. God bless melons.

The next time he saw Jeannie, Peeps stood aside to check her out, head to toe. She had a sexy posture with a face to match. She looked like she wanted a little mischief in her life and Peeps was more than happy to oblige if it came to that. She had great boobs—melons of the right size and proportion. When he finally came over to chat, he had a huge smile on his face and looked and acted very happy to see her again. They chatted for a bit, skipped further discussion on melons, and got down to business. To Peeps' surprise she asked him if he wanted to go out one evening this week. He grinned with pleasure, just like the adolescent boy he still was, and traded phone numbers and agreed to go to a French bistro on Lincoln Avenue. Peeps would make the reservations and they agreed to meet at the restaurant at seven-thirty. Jeannie absolutely insisted that they would split the bill. Reluctantly, he agreed and frankly was relieved when the bill came at the end of the evening. They had a bit of this and some of that and in the end it turned out to be an expensive meal for a first date. As they paid the bill, they both decided that the bistro was rather extravagant and that the next outing would be more modest. The great news was that there was to be another meeting; the produce manager had passed the first test.

Peeps followed Carl's long-ago advice and let Jeannie do the talking. She lived in a world that Peeps hardly knew. She went to the symphony, attended gallery openings, and regularly visited the Art Institute, of which she was a member. She spoke of studying overseas in Germany as a junior in college; Peeps for his part never went west of Western or north of Howard. Evanston was a foreign land. She mentioned neither a husband nor a boyfriend; she had no ring on her finger, which Peeps repeatedly looked at for reassurance. All through dinner Peeps just could not keep his eyes off her clothes and her breasts, and not necessarily in that order. She wore simple but classy clothes, showing a good deal of lovely skin without being risqué. She was a class act, poised, funny, and in complete control of the date. By the end of the evening, he thought he was out of his class. He was a working guy and Jeannie clearly was not. They did share one passion: a good thriller by one of the many talented contemporary authors. Oh, and she was a Cubs fan. For the moment, Marcus the wonder dog was out of work.

CHAPTER SEVEN:

Changes Afoot

It was time for Peeps to step up big time. He suggested that they go to the Art Institute on a Sunday afternoon in two weeks. This gave him time to get online and learn everything he could about the Institute's modern wing. They set a time and he went to work. He took a crash course online to relearn his high school French; he had been a good French student and was surprised how much he remembered. He spent at least an hour every night practicing phrases and working on his accent. He took lists of words and phrases to work with him to study in spare moments. By the end of the week he could name virtually every fruit and vegetable in the store. To Nanna's great surprise, he joined her to watch Antiques Roadshow and was surprised to find that he actually enjoyed the program. He and Nanna had spirited discussions about the prices for various items brought in for evaluation. Nanna, the seasoned Roadshow warrior, won the majority of the contests. Nanna also knew something was on, because Peeps was giving up prime martini drinking time at the Bubble. It will all come out, she reasoned, when the time was right. Obviously it had to be about a woman.

He loved the modern wing and Jeannie was a good teacher. She was impressed that he could read and understand texts or exhibit notes in French. They spent hours viewing and discussing the Impressionists, their works and the early twentieth century world they lived in. He surprised Jeannie ever further by asking to see the Etruscan room with its famous thousand years old mosaics. Peeps loved the symmetry and order of the pieces. They ended up closing the place and spent the next half hour looking for a place to have an early dinner. Peeps introduced her to dirty martinis and she introduced him to serious foot play under the table. By the end of the evening, Peeps was ready to sweep the plates and tablecloth off the table and have sex right there and then. He doubted Jeannie and the management would share his enthusiasm. She was taking a cab home so she walked Peeps to the Red Line, holding hands the entire time. He was rewarded with the biggest, wettest, sloppiest kiss ever. Peeps whistled all the way to the Granville stop, pissing off everyone in a very crowded train car.

One of the wonders of the age was Peeps' flip phone, recently purchased at Best Buy. The beauty was that he did not have to share the land line with Nanna. As a newbie, he spent a lot of time with the fifteen-year-old who was selling phones. He wanted to master the phone and its tricks before he left the store. The instruction booklet was slim pickings and he had to navigate the AT&T site to figure out features he had not mastered in the store. The Mates at the Bubble loved the phone; he got a great deal of shit over it; mostly the guys were jealous. He took it all in good stride. When he told his Mates that he was studying French online at night and had a date at the Art Institute, the shit really hit the fan. Who is she? What does she look like? Had he screwed her yet? Does she know he lives with his mother? The barrage of questions and insults continued until Peeps said it was time to go home and lick his wounds. He gave the group a friendly finger on the way out, laughing as he left. Guys with drinks in them would say and do anything. What fun.

How would he explain that he still lived with his mother at his age? Hmmm, this was a problem. He wondered how a sophisticate like Jeannie would react. This could be really tricky; he knew that he could not afford an apartment and still maintain the Hood St. house for Nanna. He was paying more than fifty percent of the bills, especially onerous were the ever-increasing real estate tax bills. The county and city could not wait to raise taxes; it was money carnival time with the homeowners getting the whipped cream pie in the face every six months. He had to figure this out before going out again. He decided to come clean: He helped to support his mother, he could not afford an apartment and the house, his mother was leaving the house to him on her death, and, he was a mama's boy, pure and simple. Maybe he could get a whole bunch of wine in her and she would think the story cute.

Date three did not go so well—they went to a play at the Theatre Building on Belmont; Peeps drove and they agreed to have small plates at a tapas restaurant near the theater. Jeannie declined the martini, Peeps did not. A big mistake. He could not keep awake during the performance. The theme was dark, filled with family conflict and angst. Jeannie seemed to enjoy the performance and had a good time elbowing Peeps to keep him awake. Because both had to work the next day, they called it an early evening. Jeannie said little and Peeps knew he was in the doghouse. He offered to drive her home, but she climbed into a cab. This time there was no big, wet sloppy kiss —replaced with a polite peck on the check. Driving home, he realized he knew nothing about this woman and she knew nothing about him. They never talked about family, friends, work, or interests—the usual grist for the early part of a relationship. Neither knew where the other lived. Some good old-fashioned fornicating seemed like a long shot.

While Peeps was trying to figure out Jeannie, two major events took place at the store. The cow who ran the floral department raised her ugly face again demanding to be made a manager. Peeps listened and said nothing except that he would get back to her. She ran a great department but was gruff with employees and customers. Professionally, Peeps could not afford to see thirty percent of his revenue gone with a swipe of the pen. Most of the produce department's profits came from floral. Another problem was that she was a woman in a mostly male retail environment. If the company did not recognize her work in some way, it risked a lawsuit for discrimination. He went to Terry immediately and shared the problem. Terry, the good Jesuit he was, got the issues immediately and over a beer they formed a plan. Terry came back with the news that there were only two floral departments in the entire company that had full-time managers with the title and pay to match. Both were in huge stores in Highland Park and Burr Ridge, and both were headed by women.

Peeps made appointments with both store managers and asked their advice and opinions about a separate department for floral. Over lunch, they had opposite opinions on the separation of floral from produce. One inherited the situation and found the extra manager expensive and not a full-time job. The other felt that the category had grown so large, he needed someone with knowledge and expertise to manage it. He reminded Peeps that the produce managers were typically men, who knew little about flowers. One for and one against, not much help really. He reported back to Terry and he proposed a plan: They would offer a salary increase close to what she would make as an assistant manager but without the title. Terry immediately balked at the plan, getting red in the face, saying that the woman could just walk if she did not like the current arrangement. Peeps knew when it was time to leave and said he would get back to Terry with a different plan—just as soon as he figured one out. In the meantime the cow kept the pressure up, demanding an answer or she would make trouble.

In the meantime, corporate posted a job opening for a second in command for produce purchasing and vendor selection for the entire company. It paid an astounding salary of sixty-five thousand plus an annual performance bonus. Terry suggested that Peeps apply for the job. He had the experience and had a very good track record of profitability. Part of the job was to arrive unannounced at stores to inspect the department, talk with the managers about their numbers, and how to improve performance overall. Terry reminded Peeps about two issues: First, the company preferred a candidate with a college degree, and second, that this was a clout-heavy job—he needed a strong mentor and Terry was relatively low on the store manager food chain. He had to prepare a resume, which he smartly asked Jeannie to help him write. He needed a new suit for the interviews and had to have a very strong recommendation from his store manager.

To get to the resume, he had to find out if Jeannie was talking to him. He called and asked her to go out. She was happy to hear from him and they chose a small Mexican place on Wilson, near Western. Jeannie had read an online review and thought it was worth a try. Since the conversation was going so well, he asked for her help with the resume. Terry was kind enough to give Peeps copies of resumes he had received recently so Peeps would have a model from which to work. Jeannie said yes to that, too. Two for two. She suggested that they meet at his house and work there. Peeps decided not to press his luck and he would talk about his living arrangements at dinner rather than on the phone. He wanted to see her face and body language when he told his story. That was going to be fun. Give us a boy and we will give you a man, but he is still a boy at heart. Not much progress.

He also had a solution to the flower cow. First, he spoke to the employees who reported to her and explained in general terms that the next few weeks might be difficult for them. He promised that it would not last. He arranged a meeting with the flower cow with Terry in his office. He gave Terry a general idea of his plan and he nodded his agreement. Peeps came prepared, including copies of her twice annual performance reviews. He explained that there was no opening for a floral manager or even an assistant manager. He explained that she was paid according to company standards, having just received an increase on her fifth anniversary with the company. Finally, he read off all the negative items on her reviews, which never changed. She was often rude or uncaring with customers and did nothing to help her junior associates, frequently criticizing them publicly. She had two choices: transfer to another store or she had one month to improve her people and communication skills. If she did not improve, she would be let go. Finally, he reminded her that she had no basis for a lawsuit based on her sex as she wanted a job that did not exist.

Flower cow tried to interrupt several times, but Terry intervened and said she could talk when Peeps was finished. Peeps was hard and ruthless in his management style—she deserved it and he had looked away too often. Swearing, screaming, and threats greeted Peeps when he finished. She knew he had her and it made this whole situation worse. Peeps told her in no uncertain terms that she was being insubordinate and her behavior justified firing immediately for cause. Everyone in the store heard the mayhem, customers and employees alike. Peeps had read and reread the company personnel manual last night and came with a letter informing her about when she would get her final paycheck, COBRA rights, and other pertinent information. The letter was signed by Terry and Peeps. On her way out of the store, she started knocking cans off the shelves, breaking glass bottles, and generally swearing a blue streak. Peeps, a devotee of the tavern, had never heard the word "fuck" used so creatively and so often. The head cashier had already called the police and they came in time to take hold of her before she did any further damage. Peeps next offered Laura, the only full-timer in floral, the cow's job, including salary and benefits. She accepted on the spot. Peeps told her they would start training tomorrow. Terry spent the next hour on the phone with corporate personnel wrapping up the mess. The assistant personnel manager assured Terry this went on all the time and that they did a good job managing a difficult situation.

Saturday evening was bright, cool, and generally chamber of commerce weather. Peeps got the SUV out of the garage, realizing that he had not driven it for two weeks. It was clean and bright, he was dressed casually but well, and he looked forward to a great evening. He had a hard time finding parking and knew he was a bit late—Jeannie was there waiting for a table; she knew Mexicale did not take reservations and came early to get their names on the list. They ordered margaritas, something Peeps had never tried before, while waiting at the bar for a table. Peeps noticed someone in a booth at the back of the restaurant—someone he thought he knew. He only saw the back of her head.

Once seated, with Peeps sweating up a storm, they enjoyed Mexican beer and small plates which they shared. Jeannie was right—the joint had great tacos, but also a much more detailed menu. He enjoyed the food, the company, and the conversation until he was ready to explain his domestic situation. Maybe she lived at home with elderly parents she just could not leave. Nice try. He began with his resume and that led to his confession: he simply told her his circumstances. He explained that it was financially and personally impossible to leave at this point. His mother could not handle a house by herself and needed Peeps to pay a good portion of the bills. She shrugged and said she looked forward to meeting his mother tomorrow. Peeps knew enough to talk about something else and he let Jeannie take over. He followed Carl's advice and just listened and frankly was happy to do so.

During coffee and dessert, he turned to find some woman calling him nasty names under her breath. He realized the back of the head that had seemed familiar belonged to the flower cow. Jeannie was more than startled; she seemed genuinely frightened as this crazy woman began to scream and yell at Peeps. She was behind him and he could not really turn his head to confront her. The waiter and then the owner came over and asked what the problem was. Peeps could not answer, the woman had become so loud. The cow was clearly very drunk and she had to be forced out of the restaurant. The owner, when he came back to their table, was suspicious and wanted to know what happened. The waiter translated and the owner calmed down and apologized profusely for what had happened. Jeannie wanted the dirt so he told her the whole story, including the scene at the store. He left nothing out. She was both amused and impressed. Peeps thought he might get a big sloppy tonight—or perhaps better.

They had used up their time at the restaurant, so Peeps suggested they go to her place. Jeannie said she would like to go to Montrose Harbor and continue their conversation. Peeps did not understand but got the SUV and followed marching orders. They could not drink in the park and neither wanted more coffee. They settled in the front seat with nice romantic music on—Peeps waiting to see what was what. Jeannie began by simply saying that they could not go to her place; she shared it with her husband, or rather, her ex. She had Peeps' attention. They were divorced, but the only outstanding item was their condo. Neither wanted to give it up and if she left and moved elsewhere, she would be perceived as willing to give it up. She described the condo as absolutely superb—they had bought it for a song and it was worth more than a million dollars. Peeps whistled. He did not know anyone who lived in a condo with that kind of price tag.

Peeps waited in silence, knowing there was a lot more coming. And there was a busload of shit to follow. Jeannie told the story of two hard-working people, both smart, but her ex was really bright and aggressive. They built an online and direct-to-customer employee management company specializing in firms with at least a million dollars in revenue, but not large enough to have personnel and payroll departments. When starting a business, timing is everything. Their target companies were sprouting all over the place. The business grew to fourteen million in revenue and was still growing. She owned half of it. Because of the divorce, everyone agreed she would not work full time in the office. Almost embarrassed, she admitted that she earned great money from her share of the profits. The problem was the ex.

Jeannie wanted to sell the business; they had had multiple offers at very agreeable terms. The ex did not want to sell, but because he was so distracted with the divorce, everyone—from the lawyer, accountant and their advisors—thought he should give it up. Jeannie was terrified that he would fuck up a company he worked so hard to build. She admitted that so far there had been no major screw ups, but she also felt it was a matter of time. Peeps sat in silence for five minutes trying to digest all of this. Just as he was about to say something stupid, a cop came to the door to tell them they had five minutes to leave the park. It closed at eleven and he would lock them in if they were not out in time—plus a ticket. This cop was not a happy camper; Peeps knew something about him pissed off cops. Asked what they should do now, Peeps said the dumbest of dumb statements: he suggested that they could go to the Heart of Chicago Motel on Ridge and Peterson and spend the night thinking great thoughts. Jeannie's laugh was uproarious—she told Peeps that she and the ex had spent their honeymoon at the Heart of Chicago. At the time neither had a dime to piss on.

Peeps had a backpack and an attache case and brought them in as props. They registered as Mr. and Mrs. Hollings, Jeannie's last name. Peeps was nervous as a cat in a dog pound. He sure as hell did not want to mess this up. They both were very tentative at first; Peeps had not been properly bedded in a while and did not want to be too eager and therefore sloppy. He remembered some of Carl's rules and began to undress slowly and helped her just as slowly. Half-naked, they hit the bed and began to fondle whatever could be fondled. Ever so slowly, the passion was building and very quickly Jeannie's engines went into high gear; she took charge, to Peeps' delight, and round one was an orgasmic delight. Everyone came at the right time and everyone was very pleased. What they needed after the first round was a cigarette, but neither smoked. Peeps purposely started to fall asleep, knowing for certain that they would have a loving go round in the morning. In minutes they were fast asleep. At eight thirty, they showered together and fucked like rabbits after—which meant a second shower so they both did not smell like they just got laid. After a very filling brunch, Peeps took her home to a huge and sophisticated building on Lake Shore Drive. Jeannie was not kidding about her money. Peeps suddenly felt very insecure; Jeannie sensed he was uncomfortable and chided him in no uncertain terms that he should not be concerned or preoccupied about her life and living standards. She told him straight out that she did not come from money and had to work to help pay for college. Peeps nodded and thanked her with a nice, long kiss.

They had forgotten all about his resume and he called Jeannie to reschedule for Tuesday, his day off. He agreed to mid-morning and introduced her to Nanna, who took an immediate shine to Jeannie. The women talked for about twenty minutes while Peeps prepared fresh coffee and pastries. The computer was in his so-called office, so he did not have to show her his bedroom. Everything was clean and neat and they worked for three straight hours on what turned out to be a very presentable resume. Peeps had copies of all his reviews and of his bonus information. They decided to use the flower cow incident to show his ability to manage difficult situations. Then the hard part: a convincing cover letter. Jeannie stressed that the reader would never get to his resume unless the cover was compelling.

Jeannie showed Peeps how to use the language of the job posting itself to create a letter that would demand attention. They identified five themes which had to be covered convincingly: experience, financial results, product knowledge, company philosophy and goals, and the ability to work with people he did not know and lead them to change the way they worked and managed. This took over four hours, not including bathroom breaks and lunch. As it turns out, Jeannie had been the office and hiring manager for the company she and her ex founded—until she resigned over the divorce. If he were invited for an interview, she volunteered to help him through questions and answers, what never to say, how to handle difficult questions, and how to conduct himself during the interviews. Because this was blue collar retail, she suggested a basic suit, conservative tie, and a simple portfolio to hold more copies of his resume as well as all reviews and bonus documents. What a gift, thought Peeps, and he told Jeannie outright how grateful he was for her help. He had never been through an interview before in his life. Terry spent over an hour reading and rereading Peeps' work and generally approved it. He suggested some very specific company information and insisted that after making changes, Peeps have someone with skill proofread everything. Oh, Nanna, grab your red pencil.

Sales in his store were down a bit, so Peeps spent a good deal of time struggling with the answer. He had begun training with Laura an hour a day for two weeks. They spent time on inventory and how to squeeze every dime out of her section. They decided that they would start stocking better, higher-priced plants and flowers. Instead of a bromeliad in a plastic pot, he said they should add the same plants with nice ceramic pots. Now the sale was twenty dollars instead of ten. They decided to add to the card selection; they were stocked on consignment, so they lost nothing if they did not sell. They tripled the card space so that it was noticeable. Each week they found other more profitable items and categories to add to the store. They both decided the area needed some paint and new furnishings. Terry was not thrilled, but agreed. When finished, the place looked like a spring garden. Weekly sales started up again and increased slowly for the next six months. Another item to talk about when he was interviewed for the corporate job.

In all the rush to redo his life, Peeps was not paying attention to Nanna. She was not feeling well and was having an even harder time getting on the bus to work. Peeps thought it might be time for her to retire, but was unsure how she would take it. She was still seeing Wally from time to time, but that, too, seemed to have fizzled. Then Allen fired her, in front of all the employees of the two stores. She was responsible for demise of the Winsberg retail empire. She was told to leave immediately. She was not allowed to go to the store to collect any personal items she had. Her life was over as she knew it. She had invested so much of herself in that goddamn store, she had lost her life. And for what:

terrible pay and being publicly humiliated in front of her colleagues. Allen: What a complete guttersnipe he turned out to be.

Nanna did not have time to wallow in her misery. The children did not know anything about her situation, so they came in droves with their problems. They were heavy problems. Even though the Sisters were often distant, they still expected Nanna to be both mother and advisor. Marriage crisis, talk to Nanna. Children's problems, go to Nanna. Personal crises, see Nanna. They never asked about her and whether she needed a friendly ear. The Older Sister marched in the very day that Nanna was fired, and exploded about a serious drug problem with her older son. He had been in a form of rehab twice and now they could not find him. He had disappeared with whatever money he could find in the house and had not been back. Missing persons almost laughed in her face when she filed a report. In a city of over two million, seven hundred thousand people, how the hell were they supposed to find one kid on drugs?

The very next morning, Sister Two came to the house to announce that she had stage two breast cancer and was scared as hell. Who would take care of her children: Her husband was a dumb ass, although he managed to make great money nevertheless. He could not raise the kids. She was terrified of the operation and chemotherapy that would follow. She had heard such terrible things from friends and acquaintances. She did not want to be mutilated by surgery and she did not want the pain and suffering of chemo. She had beautiful hair and she wanted to keep it. After two hours, Sister Two calmed down and went home. Peeps arrived shortly thereafter having just finished his first interview for the corporate job. He could not wait to tell Nanna. He felt that he had aced it. He was calm, clear, concise, and articulate throughout the two hours. He came up with ideas to increase revenues, including modeling Whole Foods when it comes to farm fresh and organic fruits and vegetables.

He talked on and on for twenty minutes until he realized that Nanna had heard none of it. She offered faint praise and little encouragement. Peeps could be rather thick at times, but he was at his worst this particular evening. Finally he ventured into what might be going on. Nanna did not want to talk about it;

Peeps insisted. She started to leave, but Peeps gently held her hand and begged her to sit down and talk to him.

And talk she did. All three crises came out in one big, jumbled mess. Peeps was astounded by Nanna's firing and the way she was treated. He was ready to punch the shit out of Allen. Nanna quietly reminded him that he could not get his promotion while in jail for assault and battery. Out came the Jameson; they both needed some relief from reality.

Peeps made a point of calling each of The Sisters that evening and told them about Nanna's early retirement and how it was done. He also asked and listened for more than an hour to each of The Sisters. He promised to talk to some of his Mates at the Bubble about someone to talk to in missing persons. The other Sister he had no immediate action or relief to provide except to be here for her—whatever she needed. He went next door to ask Greg for help, specifically if he knew a senior officer in the Chicago Police who he could contact and ask for help. Greg knew just the guy: a captain who drank at Bruno's on Sheridan Road, just across the street from Loyola University. Greg would make a point of going this evening and see if he was around. He also had three young grandsons he was eager to escape, for at least an hour or two. Motivations are never pure.

He tapped gently on Nanna's door, but she seemed asleep or just did not want company. Peeps got it. Even if she were awake, he doubted she would be hungry. Peeps was starving and had the bachelor's standby: ham, cheese, tomato, and lettuce on toasted rye bread with a beer. It revived his spirits remarkably. He next called Jeannie to talk about the interview, but she did not pick up. He left a message and gave her a quick rundown of the day. He grabbed another beer and went to the living room to watch television; Law and Order was on and he was happy as a clam and fell into a deep sleep. At three fifteen, he locked up the house and went to bed. Ten minutes later, as he was falling back to sleep, someone was pounding on the front door and ringing the hell out of the doorbell. Nanna was first to the door, noticing that both neighbors and the people across the street had been awakened. Nanna refused to let the man in and called 911. It turned out to be Jeannie's ex who wanted Peeps outside to murder him.

Nanna had collapsed at the door, so they could not open it. The cops were there in no time and had the ex, still ranting and swearing, locked in the back seat of the police SUV. In fact he had a gun, but no bullets and no permit, of course. He sized the ex up as he was dragged to the squad car, and Peeps thought he could pretty much take the guy. Of course he had the advantage of Greg on one side and Larry on the other. Both were big guys and could handle themselves if necessary. Now he had to explain what had just happened as far as he could figure out. The ex was more than a little pissed that he was going out with Jeannie. Peeps explained that they were divorced, or so he was told. Had Jeannie lied to him? He had no way of knowing for sure what her status was and it was not his business. He could not get to sleep after everything had calmed down, so he went to work the next day looking like the dog's dinner thrown up. He thought he looked ok when Terry finally came to work, although Terry wondered if Peeps was out late last night celebrating his interview. Terry knew the hiring manager from training they had taken together and got a phone call from her to say that Peeps was on the top of a very small list. Terry told Peeps about the phone call and he again was ecstatic; he also made the point to explain to Terry that he was not out drinking last night—just that family problems had kept him up most of the night. Terry shrugged; he just did not want to know—family counseling was above his pay grade.

Nanna settled down over the next week, focusing on her Social Security and Medicare benefits. She also needed a third-party provider which would cover most of what Medicare would not. She went next door to Greg, a pharmacy manager, and he gave her several places to go, including AARP, which she chose. She was not feeling well and a Medicare card was most important. She and Peeps settled down to review the household expenses. Peeps knew she could not pay as much, but he was fine with that. They even discussed selling the house and buying a condo on Sheridan Road. Neither were enthusiastic about selling. After talking with Social Security she was a bit surprised at the benefits. It seemed like they could go on as they had in the past. If they needed a roof or some other big expense, that was another matter. Peeps promised to add to his savings and investing to cover contingencies unforeseen.

And then there was Jeannie. He had not heard from her in days, and he refused to call every hour like a love-sick puppy. It was either on or off, he would know soon enough. Nearly a week later, Peeps got a call on his cell from Jeannie and she was crying. In between sobs, she told him that she had lied—he was not her ex but they were separated. They had spent most of last week in counseling and had decided to get back together. She apologized for the scene at his house and apologized for lying. She really liked Peeps and was sorry for the way things worked out. He deleted her number from his phone and sat at the kitchen table sobbing. He was so loud that Nanna came out to find out what was going on. Of course, she knew. He had told her that he wanted to marry Jeannie at some point. She kissed him on the top of his head, rubbed his shoulders and left him to his misery. He did not have time to feel sorry for himself. Two days later, Nanna found out that The Second Sister had stage four cancer, not stage two as predicted. The cancer had spread to her liver and lungs and she would survive for three months, tops. Peeps heard back from his captain friend and because the boy lived in Park Ridge he could not do much. He gave Peeps a number and wished him well; when Peeps called Park Ridge Police he was told he was not a person of standing in the case and that the parents had already filed for a missing person. He would not give Peeps any information about the case.

Judith Ann, The Second Sister, died three weeks later. There was no wake and no burial, at her request. The funeral mass was one of the most somber and depressing affairs Peeps ever attended. Everyone cried at the sight of the young children and the hapless father. The Brother's-in-Law parents had moved back to Chicago to help raise the kids. They would move into their son's house; there was plenty of room. They took the master suite and the father moved to one of the lesser bedrooms. After the funeral, The Grandparents made it perfectly clear to Nanna that the McAvoy family need not bother with the kids or be in touch, for that matter. Peeps had to explain to Nanna that there was no such thing as grandparents' rights. They did not exist as long as the father was alive. Stunned, she sat back on the pew and started crying all over again. She did not understand how insensitive these people could be. The Grandmother further told Nanna that her son had married well below his status. Game, set, and match.

It was no wonder Nanna never saw her daughter and the grandkids; Judy was in a situation whereby money and snobbishness overcame any reasonable family ties. She could not understand these kinds of people. They were better because they made more money and lived in the tony village of Park Ridge? And what happened to the fiercely independent daughter she once called the queen of bitches and witches in her frustration to keep some control of the girl? Had the family just sucked all of the life out of her? Was she always under the in-laws' control? Her husband certainly was too much of a mouse to control Judy when she got her Irish up. Nanna's son was dead in his late teens and now her second born was dead in middle age from cancer. Parents should not survive their children. There should be a law.

For Peeps, it was time to get to work, despite being depressed by his sister's sudden death and his concern for Nanna, particularly her health. She had to find an internist, and, in fact, he did too. But he had to get moving with the job pending. The first task was to find his replacement; the assistant manager did as little as possible and was a dolt. He and Terry huddled looking through resumes, calling friends if they knew a qualified person for produce manager, even approached managers at Jewel and some of the independent stores, including Whole Foods. They received some resumes, but neither of them were impressed with what they saw. Peeps agreed to come in on Sundays to place the stocking order for the week until Terry found someone.

In the course of these meetings, Terry gave out a very interesting bit of information. The job was posted with the lowest salary; the company did this routinely. Terry explained that there was always more money in the budget, say seven or eight thousand more. He urged him to ask about a higher salary, especially with the years of experience he had under his belt. It took two minutes with his new boss to agree on sixty-nine thousand rather than sixty-five. She just smiled at him and asked if he was ever going to negotiate. He smiled back and said he wanted to make sure it was the right time. The quick cat and mouse game over, they went to lunch for two hours; less time eating and more time going over responsibilities and strategies of whom to see first—starting with stores that were underperforming.

Peeps spent two very boring weeks at the home office going through the procedures manual, how to reprimand managers, how to establish rapport and generally how to manage the store and the produce managers. His supervisor hinted that the job was not easy and would take time and considerable effort to get to know and help the stores and their managers. Peeps was confident; he had come up through the ranks and knew his clients, he was sure. The goal was to visit three stores in the same general area, one real problem place and the others not so problematic. He started with the Englewood store, a real challenge no matter who the manager was. Impoverished for decades, there were no working- and middle-class customers for miles. Peeps, after looking at the store's numbers, decided the store would never close for political reasons. The store worked hard within the community, sponsoring job fairs, giving day-old bread and nearly out-of-date meat and vegetables to the various food pantries. They tried as best they could to hire within the community, and generally managed to do so.

But it was not a social service agency, it was a for-profit store, and Peeps had to beat this into everyone's head. When he walked into the store, he realized everyone was staring at him—he was the only white person in the place. He asked for Mr. Holmes, the manager, and a thumb sent him to the back of the store to an office which looked as though it had not been cleaned or cleared of clutter for a year — last year's Christmas specials posted on the wall were a small hint as to the status of the joint.A handshake, a grunt and a thumb sent him to see Mr. Holmes the third, affectionately called Trey. Peeps walked into what one could only call a casual work environment: an open bag of Cheetos, Cokes all around and three people chatting away without a care in the world at ten-thirty in the morning. They looked at him and he at them; he introduced himself as McAvoy, not Peeps not Mister. Just McAvoy.

No one moved until he went up to Trey, shook his hand and asked the others if they had work to do. One woman informed him that she did not work in produce and he could do nothing to her. Shaking his head, he assured her he could do something about her if he chose to push the matter. He was now alone with Trey. He tried to set a better tone by explaining he was here to help, not criticize and nitpick. The response was an open-mouthed stare. Peeps charged in with the recent numbers and talked about setting a goal of a two percent increase in sales each month for the next six months. Together they would work out the tactics to reach that goal. Peeps was willing to spend a large amount of time to help. They sat in silence for three or four minutes when Trey responded: McAvoy was the fourth white dude sent by the home office to save this store; he clearly knew nothing about the neighborhood nor the people who lived here; this store would never close no matter what happened because Dominick's could not afford the political and economic backlash if it were closed; and, there was absolutely no motivation to change anything. Peeps nodded and said out loud that their first meeting went rather well, he thought. And by the way, get the goddamn rotten fruit and vegetables cleared out before he came back later in the day. Trey was surprised by both the volume and the intensity of Peeps' comeback; he poked a finger in Trey's face and he reminded Trey who was in charge, and it was not Trey. Peeps almost ran down Holmes Sr. as he slammed out of the office with a bucket in hand to start the cleanup.

Next he went to Hyde Park, then Cicero and back to Englewood for his promised inspection. By the time he was finished, he sat in the parking lot, exhausted. He still had an hour's drive to get back to the north side. After three days of this, Peeps felt like he was a monkey trying to fornicate with a basket-ball—a lot of grunting and no satisfaction, just like a song everyone liked. He got to the weekend, and he still had to write reports and do an evaluation of both stores and managers. He slept in on Saturday, planning to use Sunday for his paperwork. He was so self-absorbed that he forgot all about Nanna and the Sister. He made plans to take Nanna to Park Ridge and visit with the family. Nanna was really anxious to be of some help, if nothing else, to show support and just listen. The older son was now listed as a sixteen-year-old runaway and there was no news, either from the police or from his friends.

On the way home, they stopped for dinner at a joint in Park Ridge; Peeps wanted martinis but knew he could have no more than two, at best, or risk a drunk-driving citation. Nanna had no such concern and managed to polish off nearly a bottle of Chianti. All the while they talked about what the other needed to do: Nanna had to get to the doctor's office; she needed to get her finances in order—she had plenty of money, as they had both forgotten about the settlement money they had in a municipal bond fund; she had to make some decisions about the house—repair it or sell it. Finally she had to get back with her friends—she needed emotional support. Peeps, for his part, also needed a doctor although he received basic check-ups every other year through the union. To his utter surprise, he needed a will. He started to argue, but Nanna was well into the wine so he lost that one. He had to figure out what he would do with his assets. The money was sure as hell not going to Judy's kids.

Once home, as it was still early, he bounced out the door to the Bubble; he was not finished drinking by a long shot. The joint was quiet for a Saturday night, although it was early. Peeps had violated his promise never to go to the Bubble on Saturday just in case an argument or two started. He was pleased to learn from Larry, the owner, that the nonsense had stopped years ago. He bent Larry's ear about his week; more than a little indifferent, Larry did introduce him to a young lawyer in private practice named Bill Barnett. They agreed to meet during the week but Peeps had to decide to whom he wanted to leave his money when he died. He also had to figure out what he actually had and put a value on the house. Sipping Tanqueray, he used the back of an envelope and came up with the astounding sum of seven hundred thousand dollars: the house was most of it, but he also had one hundred thousand in his 401(k) plan at work; over one fifty in the municipal bond fund; the rest in savings and his life insurance policy of sixty-nine thousand as long as he was still working for Dominick's. He and Barnett met at the house on Tuesday night and Peeps would leave fifty thousand each to The Older Sister's two kids. He spent time with them when he and Nanna visited; they seemed to be really good kids. He left money to several friends, even though they did not need it. The rest went to the Jesuits for training and support of new, young Jesuits. He just liked them and Terry was always a reminder of what a good group they were. Connie and Larry witnessed the will and it went on the pantry shelf, with Nanna's, behind the can of forty-year-old baked beans.

CHAPTER EIGHT:
Time Leans the Wrong Way

Peeps could not quite accept that he had just made a will. He has suffered death in the family—his father, Emmett, his brother and his sister. He had seen dozens of his friends and neighbors die over the years, gone to wakes and funerals—the usual rituals for mourning. The reality did not immediately scare him, but it did focus his attention on Nanna and her wellbeing. The old woman was particularly obnoxious when it came to discussing how she felt. When she did go to the doctor, she never shared anything with Peeps or with The Sister. Peeps felt that she was depressed and needed help, at least emotional support from people her age. Dick and Nancy lived across the street and Nanna was thick as thieves with Nancy. Her friend was sensible, kind, sharing, and religious and the two women just enjoyed each other's company. Peeps secretly plotted with Nancy to enlist her help in getting Nanna out of the house, down the street to see friends, go for lunch or just get engaged in something. He thought about changing the locks on the door, but she still owned the joint.

Nancy agreed heartily and reinforced Peeps' opinion of his mother's state of wellbeing. Fate, as it sometimes does, interjected its ugly face before the plan could be put into action. Nancy had a small stroke, and after a week in the hospital, she was home under the care of nurses Dick and Nanna. Once she politely got Dick out of the way, Nanna was at the house three or four times a day—making meals, helping with her bath, working on physical therapy—until Nancy was exhausted. After a month of frantic activity, both women were in hog heaven. Nanna had a cause and Nancy had regained almost all of her lost functions and was walking regularly with Nanna and Marcus the Wonder Dog, now slightly long in the tooth, around the neighborhood. Peeps had not had a decent meal in weeks and was told more often than not to get out of the way and get a life; she was busy. Peeps just smiled. Even after the nurse Nanna regimen was over, she had regained her spunk and interest in her family and friends. Peeps learned a great life's lesson—be involved with those around you and your life will be much better. Give us a boy and we will give you a man, redux.

With this crisis averted, Peeps had to man up to his job situation; he loved the money but hated the job. No one in the home office cared a royal crap what he did, how he spent his time. They never read the reports he worked so hard on; even worse the managers treated him like he had scurvy. Visit after visit, rarely did anything change; the departments looked the same, the managers had the same insufferable indifference to their employees and, even worse, their customers. They complained about not keeping full-time employees. He wanted to shout and take them individually by the proverbial shirt collar and beat the shit out of them. The situation infuriated Peeps; he worked his ass off for the job and it turned out the job was a real turd in the punch bowl. After five months in this job, he had only two young managers who actually wanted to learn and advance: One was a Latino lad in the Back of the Yards neighborhood—the former home of the famous Chicago Stockyards—and a white boy who had been promoted very early in the West Rogers Park area. Both were delighted to see him and he spent as much time as he could with them. He trained them on employee retention, sales growth, inventory control and a focus on profitability. These two, only, were his success stories. There were rumors that Dominick's was not doing that well, and Peeps readily understood the reasons. Management was fat and sassy and so why rock the boat.

Peeps needed some advice and made a decision; the only person he could turn to was Terry. Unfortunately, Terry had his own problems; he was a cinch to take over the much larger store in Evanston, a promotion he well deserved.

But something happened at the last minute; something serious enough to hurt a very competent and hard-working manager in the prime of his career. The rumor mill was filled with misinformation but a consistent theme seemed to be a sexual complaint—by a college student, of the male persuasion. Were this true, there might be something hinky about these Jesuits after all. Jesus, Peeps thought, sex with a guy when Terry was married with teenaged boys of his own. He decided to give him a break and refused to accept all the crap that was floating around. He talked to friends about what they had heard, but it all came out the same. There could be no police action for molesting a boy; the guy was over twenty and his only recourse was to sue for damages in civil court, if it came to all of that.

Peeps set his strategy by making an appointment for his bi-monthly visitation, with Terry and his produce manager. The produce manager was not very good and had mediocre reviews, at best. His volume was down and his profits were down further. He was an easy mark and everyone knew it, including the produce manager himself. Peeps was sure that he was very nervous about the evaluation and should be. In Terry's office, they talked about old times and agreed to go for lunch after Peeps castrated his produce manager. The fact is, Terry took a certain delight in the guy's misery because he knew Peeps would not be kind or sympathetic. Peeps knew this guy's job and the guy knew it. Peeps was hugely successful in his former position. Because Peeps was ready to settle in for the long haul, he chose a restaurant far away from the store in Evanston. He wanted Terry relaxed and as comfortable as he could be given the various pressures he was under.

They both ordered drinks—both knew they were not going back to the office, as it were. They talked about everything under the sun until lunch was served. Peeps decided to ask what had happened and could he be of any help? Peeps knew it was always better to ask to be of help before asking for help. Terry confessed that he planned on asking Peeps to take over the Evanston store with him, at the very least as produce manager and more likely as an assistant manager. Peeps was thankful and that led to the obvious elephant in the room: What had happened? Terry was a shoo-in for Evanston. He had barely taken a bite before Terry broke out in tears, sobbing like a child. His life was ruined, his reputation was damaged forever. His wife was talking divorce, although they were fairly strict Catholics. His sons would not speak to him; they would not even sit at the same table with him. He had lost fifteen pounds, was drinking like the proverbial fish and was depressed, to the point of being under a doctor's care.

There was some good news, if it could be called that. The company had decided to protect him from civil damages and made a monetary settlement with the employee. In that sense, Terry was off the hook. He was also told he would not lose his job—he might not advance as planned, but he would have a living. Peeps had no suggestions what to do with the wife and kids. That definitely was above his pay grade. Peeps offered his family room in the basement if matters really turned to shit. Peeps also reminded Terry that many customers who came to the Broadway store were gay; he needed to keep a low profile and until this part of the community had their say, he could only hope that some gay customers might say that Terry was set up. Peeps promised to talk to his gay friends at the Bubble, particularly one guy named Charles, who was generally accepted and used his time at the Bubble to find customers for his Allstate insurance business a few blocks away. The opinion of one was better than nothing.

Terry, exhausted from his woes, asked Peeps what was up. Peeps described what he thought was a terrible job and why. Terry did not seem surprised. He asked Peeps straight out if he could afford a salary cut to come back to the retail level; he assured Terry that he could. The money was great but the job was extremely frustrating and sucked big time. He found it difficult to get up in the morning, and to face the empty-headed, indifferent crowd day after day was mind-numbing. He could have a better conversation with a cabbage head than with the majority of the produce managers under his supposed care. Terry would speak to the one person in human resources who still liked him to arrange for a demotion and subsequent pay reduction as soon as Peeps gave him the go ahead.

On the third drink, Terry told Peeps that the company was having trouble. Ever since Mr. Dominick died, the company seemed rudderless. Aldi had come to Chicago and was nibbling at the low end; Jewel, or Jewels as it was affectionately called in the working-class neighborhoods, had suddenly found new life—offering prepared foods and less canned and frozen products. Another new player, Whole Foods, was growing rapidly in the suburbs and wealthy neighborhoods in the city. And then there were Target and Walmart. Every managers' meeting complaints and bitching filled the agenda. No one in senior management seemed to recognize the problem, or if they did, had a clue as to what to do. Dominick's, in management's view, would always be this quaint, folksy neighborhood grocer who sold what customers wanted, even if they did not know what they wanted.

So the two wise men decided that Peeps would give two weeks' notice and return to the store level; Terry would hire him at the highest rate possible—as it turned out, Peeps was docked only three thousand a year. Terry would play cloistered nun for six months to see how the wind was blowing, and Peeps would discuss the matter with his substantial contacts within the gay community. Peeps made an appointment with his supervisor and tried to explain why he wanted out; she could care less. The position had been open for nine months before Peeps took it and there were no other candidates when he applied. She left the room without even a handshake or good wishes. Nanna, one time in anger, had referred to his sister Judy as the queen of all bitches and witches. Peeps was pretty sure she outdid his sister in spades. Nasty, nasty. Peeps left the meeting absolutely convinced that he had made the right choice.

Terry made the other produce manager disappear by some magic and Peeps took over on Broadway. The good news: He did not have to travel to places where Jesus lost his sandals; the bad news was that he forgot how tiring day to day management could be. He came home every night and soaked in scalding hot water to relieve the pain in his legs and thighs. He would get into store shape soon enough; sooner was better than not. While all of this was going down, he finally had a decent dinner in Park Ridge with The Sister and Nanna. He told them what he had done and why. Only The Brother-in-Law spoke and he was more interested in Dominick's than Peeps' work change. Peeps was not sure why, but The Brother-in-Law tried to pump him for more information about Dominick's. Peeps stopped talking and brought up the hapless Cubs as an alternative.

After talking to Nanna, Peeps agreed to house Terry for a few months, at fifty dollars a week for room and board. It was a gift that Terry greatly appreciated. Terry and Wife would probably not get a divorce—neither wanted one—so they would separate. They would sell the big house in Ravenswood Manor and the Wife and kids would find a smaller, cheaper house. They would split the sale sixty for the Wife and forty percent for Terry. The house sold so quickly, at nearly full asking price, the family was almost homeless. They went to live with a sister in Elk Grove Village until she could find a house. She needed one in her old neighborhood and at something she could afford. While their relationship was very frosty, Terry did his best to help on the house, moving, getting a mortgage and all of the rest of the crap separation meant.

Peeps did his very best to stay out of it except to listen and make the introductions to his Mates at the Bubble. Both were very careful to keep personal lives away from the store. Something Peeps noticed was a gradual change in the story line about that sexual encounter with the young man. Many in the loop felt that Terry was set up, probably for money. Terry seemed to almost believe that this is what had happened and started to change narrative to fit that interpretation of the facts. Peeps knew he had already begun using the new version with his kids and wife. Terry also went to therapy to discover if he were gay or even bi-sexual. He went so far as to go to gay bars and to interact with guys and see if he really wanted to be part of that scene. This discovery process went on for months and in the end both Terry and therapist, Dr. Carney, thought he was bisexual, equally comfortable with men and women. Terry shared this with Peeps only under very discreet circumstances. Peeps gave a solemn vow not to discuss Terry or his mess with anyone. Peeps kept this promise to his dying day.

To ensure that life would not be boring, Nanna started on him about a girlfriend. She told him he was getting older and not the catch he once was. Soon he would need those little blue pills. Peeps wondered if Marcus the Wonder Dog used little blue pills. He knew that Nanna's bluntness was not without love. She did not want him to live in old age without a woman, someone who loved him and would guide him—and of course nag him as necessary, usually about once a week. Peeps spent more and more time on the floor of the store and more time interacting with customers. Terry almost laughed out loud, he was so obvious. But he did understand. In fact over the next six months Peeps met several very nice ladies, but none of them were interested in anything but a roll in the hay. Peeps certainly did not reject these good times and did get some little blue pills just in case. He also brought Marcus the Wonder Dog out of mothballs, for when the weather got better. He would focus on the beaches and take his chances. Who knew, he might have some success. Meanwhile, Nanna went on a rampage herself, talking to friends and neighbors for suggestions and blind dates. Peeps got word of this and was really pissed at his mother. He told her in no uncertain terms to cease and desist. *Alea iacta est*—the die was cast. Peeps had more dates and coffee chats than he could manage. A dozen women came and went, many divorced with kids. Peeps thought he was too old and ill-prepared to manage someone else's kids.

The gods were finally good to him and Peeps did have coffee with Christy, a trim blonde and blue-eyed beauty at least ten years his junior. She did not seem to mind; she was legally blind and physical appearance made little difference to her. Christy was a cousin of someone in the neighborhood, but Peeps could not keep it straight. She was never married and worked as a social worker for the City of Chicago's Department of Aging. Peeps learned on their first so-called date that she lived by herself on Sheridan Road at the Edgewater Beach Apartments, the iconic "pink building" which was once part of a hotel complex, so named because the Outer Drive did not exist then and the building's boardwalk extended to the water's edge. The finest resort area in the city in its day, everyone famous in the thirties, forties and fifties stayed at this complex.

Peeps did not think the coffee went well; he did not get her phone number, although she took his. He was distracted by the fact that she was handicapped; he had never sat down and had a conversation with someone who was disabled, although she seemed comfortable and outgoing, promising to stop at the store to see him. It was extremely difficult to understand how someone could manage being blind so easily. She was independent, seemingly in every aspect of her life. She was by definition careful when out in public and Peeps understood perfectly why: Without sight, she missed body language, facial expressions and even posture most people used to judge social situations. Not sure if this would go anywhere, Peeps realized that he would have to go very slowly and he would have to learn to accept Christy for exactly who she was.

She did not call and she did not stop in the store. Well, the weather was getting better and both he and Marcus the Wonder Dog needed exercise; off to Montrose beach and harbor for some serious women watching. But in fact she did call; she left a message on the landline, and as neither Nanna nor he ever checked messages, he discovered her lovely voice asking to go for lunch on Saturday. Sadly, Saturday had come and gone by a week. She did leave her number, oh glorious joy! It took another day to get a hold of her and he explained to his complete embarrassment what had happened. She told him that she lost his cell number and dialed 411 for a phone number. They both laughed nervously and agreed to Sunday brunch, the only day that they each had off.

They agreed on Calo, the place where most of Peeps' romances had begun— and sometimes ended. It was a safe place for her, always crowded and where people knew each other well. He offered to pick her up, but she insisted that she would just walk over from her apartment; what was that about? Walk over? She clearly had a mind of her own and she was not afraid of life. Peeps really liked that: No whining about her fate and the raw deal life presented. Besides her good looks, she seemed open and sincere; she was not encumbered with children and past marriages that had gone wrong. He thought that he would have to be very careful and not offer to do too much or impede her independence. He really thought that this kind of chauvinistic behavior, which he was quite capable of, would end this relationship before she had a chance to find out what a real catch Peeps was. Give us a boy and we will give you back a dreamer.

Lunch on Sunday seemed to go well; he tried to use the Carl axiom of ensuring that the lady did the talking; but she would have none of that. In truth after an hour and one half he knew next to nothing new about her. He talked like a magpie, about his family, sharing a house with Nanna, his work, his love of martinis and in general his tendency to read history, biographies, and the latest thrillers. He spent a lot of time talking about his love of Chicago history and how, when he retired, he was going to spend time reading and researching the city he loved so much. Finally, exhausted and with most of his pasta still uneaten, he apologized for being such a jerk and talking too much. Christy laughed and told him frankly she was advised by a friend long ago to get the guy to talk about himself rather than monopolize the conversation. Peeps wondered if Carl had a sister.

Strangely, their next date was a movie at the 400 on Sheridan. Again he offered to pick her up and she declined. It was just as well; parking was a complete bitch anytime and worse on Saturdays. She cabbed and he walked. He was not sure how this was going to work; she sensed his confusion — Peeps' voice gave him away every time. He was about as subtle as a truck driving through a rock concert. They settled down with very greasy and salty popcorn and drinks—her choices—and she explained that she would periodically ask him to describe the scene in a few short words so as to not disturb others around them. She told Peeps that she listened to books on tape all the time and was very good at filling in the details in her imagination. They practiced their whispers which meant that Peeps got close enough to enjoy her body and her scent. He got the shivers.

On the way out, Peeps ducked into the men's room, did his business, and went to the sink to wash and take a little blue pill, just in case. When he finished washing his face and looked into the mirror to find two guys about his age laughing their collective asses off. Grinning like crazy, the one guy slapped him on the back and told Peeps to have a great time. The three left the room laughing with big grins on their faces. Christy asked what he was laughing about and all Peeps could stammer was a joke someone told in the loo. He beat Christy to the punch by saying that the joke was not appropriate to repeat and was glad she could not see the lie on his face or his embarrassment. Fortunately, she let it go; it turns out she had three older brothers and knew exactly what men could be like. The moment passed quickly and Peeps started to look for a cab;

Christy suggested that they walk down to Bruno's for a drink. Peeps seconded the plan and took her hand and headed off to the most famous watering hole in Rogers Park. The place was mobbed with students buying in bulk from the front of the store and the older people seated and standing in every nook in the bar. She ordered Jameson's and a chaser; ditto for Peeps. Within minutes they were seated as patrons gladly gave up seats for Christy and her date. They met Peeps' friend and next-door neighbor Greg; as he was on his way out he stopped for introductions and an offer for a round of drinks. They both declined and as Peeps looked over toward Christy, Greg gave Peeps the ok sign with a big grin. Men are such pigs; you would think the only thing on their minds was sex. Thank God Peeps was above that.

After drinks, they spent ten minutes looking for a cab—he assumed for her. When she got in she asked him with a straight face if he wanted to see her etchings. Etchings. Yes, etchings. He stood there foolishly until she grabbed his hand to pull him in while the cab driver crabbed that he had to make money and some stupid guy was just standing in the street not recognizing the clear signs for a very pleasant evening ahead of him. The cabbie kept grumbling and Peeps reminded him that they could have ordered an Uber and the more he bitched the less the tip. That shut him up. They arrived at the Edgewater Beach, still talking about etchings and laughing like crazy; they got out of the cab, up the stairs and Peeps tripped on the threshold of the main door, while Christy glided right over it. What a clod you are McAvoy; he kept banging his head with his hand until they got to the elevator.

On the way up, she put her hand in his pants pocket—nothing more. Peeps thought he would melt. He kissed her on the check; go slow, go slow, Carl whispered. Let her take the lead, Carl coached. Relax and enjoy the evening, Carl suggested. Peeps had to look up Carl Valenti when he had a chance—these days you could find anyone if you just knew where to look. When she opened the door to her flat, Peeps saw a very sparse room with little furniture. He got it immediately; less was absolutely more. Less to trip over, less to bang kneecaps against and because she could not see, what was the point of art and pictures. Peeps, completely in the spirit of the evening, demanded in no uncertain terms to see the famous etchings. The silence held for ten seconds before they both fell on themselves laughing. Peeps kept at it: Where are the goddamn etchings? He was here under false pretenses. He demanded justice.

He got justice. And was it sweet. Christy grabbed him by the belt buckle and told him in no uncertain terms to undress her slowly; she wanted slowly. Sweet Jesus, little blue pills made no provision for slowly. He wanted to scream but followed directions as best he could. He apologized for not going slower, but Christy did not seem to mind. Tomorrow will be different, she told him. But he had a more pressing problem; he had to go to the bathroom and there were no lights on. Why would a blind woman have lights on? No reason. He struggled out of bed so as not to disturb Christy and then prowled the corridor for the john. He cracked his shin on something and let out with a real yelp. He left the mysterious bathroom light on full throttle and went to bed, just in case he would need to find it again—and he would.

Sunday morning was just wonderful. Christy told him that there was a new toothbrush in the loo, but please after it was used, put it on the top shelf. She loved being intimate, but not that much. They had a lovely, slow romp in the hay and about ten, there was a knock at the door. Breakfast was being delivered from the cafe in the building. Peeps was impressed, extremely impressed. She had this whole thing orchestrated and Peeps was delighted to be a part of it. They ate like wolves—donuts, crisp bacon, eggs with coffee and juice. Peeps was in a whirl. He just did not know what to say, what to think. This was a dream; it was more than just sex, it was the effort of a thoughtful individual who knew what life was about. Please Jesus let this one work. He would do everything in his life to ensure a successful relationship. It was time to have a life companion, married or otherwise.

When he got home, he showered and settled to watch sports on TV. He fell asleep within minutes and only woke up because Nanna was yelling at him. He was stupid with sleep and did not understand what was going on. In two hours Nanna called him for a lovely pot roast dinner with all the fixings. Ok, so what happened two hours ago? A similar scene took place on Tuesday, Wednesday, and Friday. Peeps called The Sister to report what was going on. They literally forced her to go to the emergency room, at which Nanna made such a scene she had to be sedated. Everyone in the room knew what was going on: they sent Nanna for extensive tests the next day and reported three days later that she had advanced dementia. The projection was that if she lived for six months, it would be a major miracle. Peeps went to the chapel and cried for the better part of an hour. It came on so suddenly, but that was the nature of the disease.

Nanna did not live for six months, but six weeks. She obviously knew she was very sick and thus the reason she never talked about her doctor's visits. She put on a pretty good show, but Peeps did not recall talking or being with her that much in recent months. Peeps went over to Maloney's on Devon to make the arrangements for mass and burial. He refused to have a wake; he hated them. Irish wakes were particularly obnoxious because booze and maudlin sentiment made such a mess. The funeral would be on Saturday with an hour or so for visitation and then mass. Burial would be at All Saints next to the Old Man, for what reason he was not sure. He was cheap in the funeral arrangements and sent the rest of the money to St. Gertrude. Maloney was perfect; he arranged for a bagpiper and planned a luncheon at Calo after the burial. Peeps did not announce the Calo affair but assumed those who should be there would be there. He was not about to spend five thousand dollars, so he tried his best to keep the lunch as low key as possible. Despite the fact that Judy's family did not bother to show up for the funeral—just as well, Peeps thought—the funeral was moving and spiritual. The church was packed; even Allen Winsberg came. Peeps asked Maloney to escort him from the church—that pagan had no business at an Irish funeral, especially after the way he treated Nanna. When the piper got up to play Danny Boy there was not a dry eye in the church; the mournful melody just ate at your heart. Many of her contemporaries, all those Irish matrons, had either died or moved to assisted living. Nanna's funeral was just one more indicator that the neighborhood had changed forever.

Two days after the funeral, ladies from the hood, led by Nancy, came and cleaned out her clothes and personal effects and took them to Care for Real, a marvelous group that helped the hard up and homeless in Edgewater. Dick made three trips to get it all over to the Sheridan Road office. Care for Real put up a huge sign thanking Nanna McAvoy for her donation—a small way to recognize a kind and thoughtful woman.

Peeps told The Older Sister about the contents of the will, unsure of what her response would be. Fortunately, The Older Sister did not care much about the house; Peeps suspected that she did not know that the value of the house was much more than she suspected. So they agreed to meet at the house with Bill Barnett and go over the particulars. Barnett was fairly certain that the non-real estate assets would have to be shared with Judy's family; it would go to them through her estate. Had Peeps known that she was so sick, he would have asked Nanna to change it in favor of The Older Sister only. Barnett pointed out that such a change would have been challenged in court and would probably not have helped; they would challenge her ability to be rational enough to make a new will. It frosted his balls that those effete snobs would benefit from a hard-working woman's life savings. He begrudged them even so much as a nickel.

Peeps took a week of bereavement, a benefit his company granted with pay, to handle the title to the house, notification to Social Security and the Policeman's Benefit Association, canceling credit and debit cards and dozens of other small items. The utilities had to be transferred to him and he exhausted himself throwing out old furniture—he bought a new king-sized bed—and painted his and Nanna's rooms. Christy was a real champ throughout; she even took her turn at painting, with some direction from Peeps. He could have finished in two hours without her help, but was so taken by her sincerity that he let her help. A blind woman painting—The Mates at the Bubble would love that one.

He and Nanna had talked recently about renovating the kitchen and bathrooms; with Christy in tow, he went to Home Depot and contracted with them to do the work. He spent hours picking out cabinets, tile, flooring and fixtures, all the while describing everything in detail for Christy. The team from the design department were great, making wonderful suggestions with an effort to keep within a budget. He insisted that they use plastic to keep the mess out of the rest of the house. He did not want to return to his house with a coating of plaster dust everywhere. Peeps did not have a budget, he just did not want to spend so much that it was out of proportion to the value of the house. He handed over his credit card for the ten thousand dollar down payment like he was buying a six pack of beer. He must be really fucked up. Christy, the absolute angel, offered her place when the construction was hot and heavy. Peeps hoped hot and heavy would be the general theme of this visit. He just could never get his mind off his dick; his mother had just died and this is what he was thinking about. Give us a boy and sometimes you get a boy back. Oops.

The remodeling and Peeps visitation with Christy went generally well, except for the wrong tile in the bathrooms and mismatched cabinets in the kitchen. All were corrected with no harm done. Living with Christy day to day was a real eye-opener. He was a bachelor and never spent more than a day with a woman; it was now going on to two weeks and they had not bitten each other's heads off. In fact, they managed to get along just fine. Peeps thought this was very promising. They split up chores, with Peeps volunteering to do the cooking; Christy accepted immediately, as she admitted she was not much of a cook. Peeps, for his part, had gotten much better because Nanna did less and less before she passed. Mornings were chaos because neither were used to sharing a bathroom. Peeps started taking showers at night to relieve the morning goat fuck.

When he moved back to his house, he was almost immediately overcome with mild depression. He was so busy, he had not had the time to fully mourn. He missed his mother desperately and hated living in the house by himself. He found himself spending more time at the Bubble and drinking much more than usual. The Mates and Larry noticed the changes and kept a close watch on him. While Terry still came to the Bubble, he had moved back home months ago and went through extensive family counseling. The family reunited in short order, Peeps was delighted. Terry had spun the tale that he was set up by this young guy, repeated the line so often, he even convinced himself that was what happened. At the same time, he worked on his reputation at work. New human resources people had come in and Terry worked with them to update his personnel jacket. His star also went up because his store had the best year in its history and management had short memories and focused on the fact that this guy knew how to sell groceries. Peeps got a six thousand dollar bonus—three times his best effort. But none of this helped Peeps. He was not eating, and lost a bunch of weight and spent his free time moping around the house, unfocused and undisciplined. One Tuesday, Terry and Larry took Peeps' martini away and told him as bluntly as they could that he needed professional help. Christy just happened to be there that evening as well.

Terry made an appointment with Dr. Carney, the therapist he had seen, drove Peeps to his first appointment, and waited to take him home. Nothing was said and nothing needed to be said. Terry kept up the chauffeuring until he was convinced that Peeps would continue his sessions. In two weeks, with the help of some medication and talk therapy, Peeps made great strides. Christy cheered him on and embraced him emotionally as much as possible. She even agreed to attend one session during which he admitted that he was madly in love with Christy. She cried, Peeps bawled, the therapist cried. After another three months, the therapy was over except for a supply of anxiety pills which did marvels helping him cope with everyday reality.

CHAPTER NINE:
Ecstasy and Agony

After several months, Peeps asked Christy to be his wife; she agreed immediately and had to help Peeps off his knee. Then they went ring shopping. They went down to the Jeweler's Building on Wabash, by far one of the largest buildings in the world devoted to the wholesale and retail jewelry trades. The building was a huge 19th century edifice filled with hundreds of small stalls and well-publicized retailers. They chose the first floor Chicago Jewelry Exchange for its vast inventory and seemingly reasonable prices. They went on a Sunday so they could take their time. They found a three-quarter carat ring set in platinum and they bought silver wedding bands, very simple and dignified. Peeps had three thousand dollars in cash and asked Christy to visit other stores while he haggled with the owner. And haggle he did; he left the store two times only to have the owner drag him back. It took about an hour, but he managed to pay twenty-six hundred dollars for the entire stash. The rings were sized while they waited and when he left, the jeweler swore at him in Yiddish. Peeps smiled and was proud of himself.

Peeps and Christy never talked about whether she wanted a church wedding or should they just go downtown to get married by the county clerk. He did find out that Christy had an older brother who she wanted at the wedding, perhaps to walk her down the aisle—assuming they got married at St. Gertrude. He had to explain that they would have to attend marriage classes and Peeps would have to register as a parishioner. He was hardly active in the parish, even though

Nanna was very much so. They went over to the church and Christy just loved it. The church was a plain building on the outside but had marvelous stained-glass windows which lit up the inside. The main aisle was long and narrow with pews on either side. The ceiling and its ornamentation were painted in various hues of blue. It was gorgeous in its simplicity. They picked a date with the parish secretary and met with the pastor who would marry them. They liked the idea of a fall wedding and that would give them more time to get to know each other.

Wedding invitations were a bit tricky; they did not want to spend their life savings so that their friends and family could get drunk and stupid. Most of the people on the list were Peeps' family and friends. Christy added ten or so people, including the mysterious brother. Christy got a list of reception halls from her friend at work who was just married. They decided to go with the friend's choice; Christy assured Peeps the place was great and the price was just right. They also engaged her caterer, disc jockey, and photographer. Within a week, Christy had moved into the Hood Street house and spent her evenings learning her way around. Peeps got rid of any small crap that might get in her way; he had to learn not to leave shoes at the front door or move furniture around needlessly. It was a big learning curve—and Christy was there to remind him in no uncertain terms he had to change the way he lived. After a few sharp rebukes, Peeps got into the spirit and was absolutely scrupulously careful—until the next time.

Christy had to decide what she wanted to do with the condo—which she owned outright, much to Peeps' surprise. She decided to sell rather than be a landlord. Peeps called up Daniel Otto to engage him as an agent to sell the property. Daniel was a neighborhood guy who lived on the fifteen hundred block of Glenlake. He was honest as the day is long and could be counted to offer sound advice as to market value and changes they should make before putting the unit up for sale. Christy followed Peeps lead on the real estate deal; she knew he always paid attention to what was selling and for how much in the neighborhood. Peeps wanted the condo sold before they married so that it was not common property, but solely Christy's. He explained that this money was hers alone and should be her slush fund and security blanket. Once they were married, however, Peeps would rewrite his will and make her a joint owner of the house; upon his death and as his spouse, she would inherit the rest of his assets, which like magic, had grown substantially. During a hazy evening discussion on money, one of his Mates explained in detail the time value of money and the sooner in life you invested the more you would have in the end. Wonderful concept, he marveled.

Daniel had the condo painted and arranged with Bob Cox, the best local tradesman anyone knew, to repair this and that. They spent about four thousand, including having the hardwood floors redone—a sum they both thought was very reasonable. Peeps assured Christy how beautiful the place looked; it sold for five thousand less than asking price. It took two months. Everyone was amazed by the speed and the lack of screwing around the transaction took; it was priced to sell, the floors looked great and the inspection went through without a hitch—Christy had to replace a shower nozzle - that was it. There were congratulations all around. Daniel made a nice fee; Christy did not have to worry about renting the condo and being a landlord and she had cash in the bank to help pay for the wedding.

Peeps had to force himself back to reality. He had not talked to The Sister for over a week and felt like a real jerk for not checking in with her. For over an hour, he listened as she alternately talked and cried; the bottom line was that she had no new information at all. The case had gone cold, as the coppers say. Peeps suggested that they put up a reward, say five thousand dollars, for any information. The police did not like the idea, but the family went ahead anyway; they also hired a retired cop named Lancy who was a private detective—he actually owned a small firm with about a dozen people working for him. He needed three thousand to even open the file, but The Sister and Brother-in-Law felt it was all worth the money spent. Peeps put in two thousand and Christy very graciously did the same. Peeps joined his family at the first meeting and listened carefully, asked lots of questions and took copious notes. If this was going to happen, it would be done right; the McAvoys were not chumps to fall victim to some sleaze. After the meeting, they all felt comfortable with Lancy. The flurry of activity was exhilarating and hopeful. Where the hell would a sixteen-year-old kid go?

Christy set a time to meet her brother, Ralph Bunch, for dinner at Gene &
Georgetti's Steakhouse for a Wednesday night get together—one of the oldest,
finest, and most expensive joints in the city. It seems Ralph was a regular and had
the privilege of a first-floor table; the common people had to climb the stairs to
the second floor, a remarkably dark and sinister hall where the all-male, middle
aged servers vied with each other to be as rude and unpleasant as possible. It was
a remarkable concept: Abuse the customers and they will come back in droves
to buy overly priced steaks with the least amount of service possible. The joint
was an institution and a place where movers and shakers moved and shook the
city. By the time they got there, paid a fortune to park, with the assumption
that he would have to pay the bill, Peeps was in a bit of a funk. He was tired
and really wanted to be closer to home. On the other hand, it was important
to Christy and so important to him.

He rallied when he finally met the much-talked-about Ralph—a man of
at least sixty, with his tie down and wearing the sloppiest suit one could imagine. The suit and the dry cleaners must exist on different planets; the tie was
made to match, with gravy stains plentiful. Ralph was on his third Manhattan
and about to order another when they arrived. His opening salvo was that he
was surprised Peeps was going to marry his sister, the slut. Peeps gawked and
started to grab him by the throat; Christy put her arm on Peeps and held him
back. She just smiled and explained that Ralph was still pissed that their parents
had left her the family money and almost nothing to her brothers. The fact that
old Ralphy, as she called him, had more money than god still did not matter.
Besides, she justified, she was the baby and by far the best-looking of the bunch.

Old Ralphy was not to be put off so easily; he informed Peeps in no uncertain terms that if you Googled Christy Bunch the search would mention nothing but her notorious reputation as a high-class hooker, one with a following
a mile along. Her kinky appeal, he insisted, was the thrill of having sex with a
blind woman. She even had her own web page, he insisted. (Peeps could not
contain himself when he got home; openly, in front of Christy, he did the search,
and yes there was an escort service under her name: Bunch's Bunnies). Christy
did not miss a beat and asked how the fourth wife was and had she spent all of

his considerable money yet. Ralphy mumbled something about her being mean as a snake and focused on his cocktail. Peeps finally got a word in and asked if he could have his sister in marriage—in lieu of a father. Ralphy burst out laughing, spilling his drink down the front of him. Marry the whore he said, a little too vigorously, causing half the room to look in their direction. The other half knew Ralph and paid no attention at all. Christy then asked him to walk her down the aisle at the church and please be sober. Peeps requested, with no little malice, that a clean suit and tie would be nice as well. Ralphy wanted to know what this church business was all about; he got the shortened version from Peeps and explained it as a long-held Irish tradition. You are marrying a Mick, again for everyone in the room to hear. Best fucking race in the world, was Peeps' retort.

The evening turned out to be very pleasant despite the round of insults in the beginning. Peeps had the best bone-in ribeye ever imagined; he thought of licking the plate and could not remember when he had eaten so much. Christy monopolized the conversation by telling stories of her family growing up in Indiana and about her brother, the highly respected divorce lawyer; he had made a fortune defending rich men who wanted to keep their money. Ralphy had a reputation as a nasty litigator and even tougher negotiator; he never took women as clients. He was a chauvinist of the first order, and wore his pig pin proudly. In true fashion, he found few women with the money to pay his ridiculous fees. Besides the cash, he felt a fellowship with every male who was about to be taken to the cleaners by a bitchy wife. Peeps could not imagine why he was married for the fourth time—he was such a gentleman. He was most proud of his own three divorces. He did not represent himself but used a female lawyer who was as outrageous as he was. Peeps wondered if the Jesuits could even manage him; he doubted it.

Save the date cards, as had become the tradition, were sent and the couple expected sixty people for the wedding reception. He had asked his friend Greg and his boss Terry to stand up for him. Christy asked two girl friends for her side. Peeps did not want to rent tuxes and both guys were relieved; it was ridic-ulous for men of their age to go prancing around in formal wear; younger guys did that sort of thing. They spent one entire evening sending checks or calling in charge card numbers to the various vendors; most wanted half with the rest due before the wedding. Christy paid for almost all of the deposits; she explained that she had the cash and why pay interest on charge cards. They next talked about a honeymoon; Europe was considered, but in the end they decided on a trip to Quebec and Montreal—it would be prime season and the country and the cities were grand. Peeps spent three evenings working on their itinerary, constantly consulting Christy. They would fly into Montreal, visit for three days, and take the train to Quebec City; every online site raved about the train and what a great experience it was. They would return to Montreal for two days and head home. They both needed copies of their birth certificates and took care of that the next Tuesday, Peeps' usual day off.

He was slacking off at work, but got back to it once most of the plans were finalized. What could his boss say; after all, he was the best man. Sales had slipped a bit during the early summer, although profits were steady. He had to figure out why sales were down; it did not take long to find blame with their vendors. Dominick's was hurting a bit and the solution was to buy cheaper, but customers noticed. Further many of these vendors were not organic producers, and that was all the rage. Whole Foods was ramming this down everyone's throat and it was working. Peeps complained to Terry and insisted that he spend an hour or two in the produce department to inspect inventory as it came in. Fortunately, Peeps as a senior manager, had the right to reject shipments that he thought unacceptable; and he exercised his veto vigorously. Terry really solved the problem by showing Peeps how he could go offline and buy from vendors approved by corporate but not on the official list. He was particularly pleased with a medium-sized group based in Michigan.

Peeps went to work on the signage in the store, announcing at every turn that the store had new inventory; he did not announce that prices were five percent higher. But that did not seem to faze his Edgewater neighbors, who were increasingly more affluent than ten years ago. Sales went up ten percent and profits by a whopping eighteen percent. Peeps expected serious feedback from corporate, but as the numbers came in week after week, no one said a word. Terry just smiled and loved the way Peeps once again pulled a rabbit out of the hat—a gift of his Jesuit education, he was sure.

Again back to reality; it was three weeks since the family met with the private detectives. The Park Ridge police gave the private eyes every lead that came in from the reward campaign, they wanted nothing to do with it and resented the private eyes for their involvement in the case. They, of course, had done nothing for months, so no one cared about the police. The file was dumped in cold case and was not touched. No one cared, except the increasingly depressed parents. This was just another junked up kid who went to the gutter; they had more important matters—particularly catching speeders on Devon Avenue. The Sister demanded the police file and was refused repeatedly; in total frustration she turned to her brother for help. They needed a bulldog and he just happened to know one—good old Ralphy.

Peeps made an appointment with Ralphy; he immediately wanted to know if Peeps could pay his fees for the forthcoming divorce. Peeps reminded his brother-in-law that he was not yet married and certainly not in need of a divorce lawyer. Crestfallen, Ralphy asked what was what. Peeps explained with a straight face that he needed a prick and asshole to assist his sister; Ralphy took this as a supreme compliment and yelled to Rachel, his paralegal and hugely abused employee, to come in. The meek woman showed up with shoulders slumped and face drawn; she looked like she had been abused by her employer for decades, yet came back for more. Peeps explained what they were about with this boy and that they wanted the police file, which was not forthcoming. They needed leverage and they needed someone tough to get the goddamn file. Would he help, at no fee of course? The paralegal winced even before Ralphy let out a string of expletives that would make a marine proud.

The paralegal, with typical abuse, was sent to her office to research the law and get back to him before the afternoon; she said nothing. Ralphy took out a bottle of very old and vintage Irish whiskey and poured shots for both of them. They toasted the Irish monks that created such a marvel and drank it down. Then they got down to business; of course, he would help. He loved fucking with the suburban police; they were such dweebs, they knew nothing and did nothing. Ralphy admitted that he was unsure if he could get the file but was happy as a clam to kick some ass and create as much misery as he could. After all, he was an officer of the court and drank regularly with a number of Cook County judges, many of whom owed him a favor or three. He asked about the private dicks they had hired and generally approved; they were good, not great, but fine for this operation. He cautioned not to pay too much without serious proof of progress. Another round of shots sealed the deal. As he was leaving, Ralphy explained that he had a very good relationship with Margaret, the paralegal; she received twenty percent of every fee they billed and was a very wealthy woman in her own right. Further, despite appearances, she could be a real bitch.

Thankfully, Peeps had taken the Red Line down to the Loop; even as a serious drinker, he was not used to shots at ten in the morning—although he admired the whiskey very much. He wondered if the Bubble stocked such a gem. Speaking of the Bubble, he was far behind in his martini drinking and had promised himself to cure this ailment. Larry even threatened to pull his gin from the ice bin; this would be a terrible slam to his reputation as a goof-off. How to reconcile time at the bar with being married. This could be tricky; he had to plan a strategy good enough to satisfy the wife. So far she said little, but that could easily change. He was fairly certain that Christy would go to the Bubble once in a while, but not regularly. He just did not see her as a bar flyette. What would a Jesuit do? He should consult Terry, the wise man.

Terry's solution was to stake out Peeps' time early on and set the precedent for after they were married. He pointed out to Peeps that he got home hours before Christy came home; she had no choice but to take public transportation and Peeps only had to walk across the street, after shopping for dinner, to enjoy his cocktails. This he did three or four days a week. He never stayed so long as to be late in preparing dinner, which he almost always did. They were usually simple meals, meat, rolls, a vegetable, and more frequently, fresh fish at Christy's request. He rarely had fish growing up, except Fridays in Lent, but began to enjoy the change from beef or chicken. He was particularly fond of Arctic Char and Lake Superior whitefish. He copied recipes from the internet and tried different marinades. Sunday they always went out for an early dinner at one of the local joints. After a couple martinis he was more than willing to listen to Christy talk about her day and clients. The stories were sadly depressing; being poor and old in a big city could be very jarring just to survive. Almost every evening he silently prayed for Christy's people and thanked God that they were not in those circumstances. Poor health, old age, and poverty were overwhelming and fed on each other to make life miserable.

Christy went to bed early because of the time it took her to prepare for the day and commute to work. Peeps constantly worried about her commute and tried to figure out a way to drive her; their schedules would not allow this. Snow and ice on the ground were her real nemesis; Peeps knew she fell one or twice a month during the bad months, although she never spoke about it. By arrangement, Peeps went to bed early so they had time for the all-important part of life—sex, glorious sex. They had grown very compatible and very passionate in their love-making. She was always enthusiastic and Peeps always followed Carl's Rules of the Bedroom, which had served him well all of these years, and he saw no reason to abandon it at this late date. One odd part of sharing a king-sized bed with Christy was that he was always slightly uncomfortable about sleeping in the same bed. He was just used to sleeping alone

The wedding was two weeks away, and the Mates at the Bubble put the pressure on big time. Did he really want to get married? She would have a ring in his nose in a month. He would never be seen at the Bubble again. They called him lover boy and what did this pretty young woman see in an old shit like Peeps. Did he know what to do on the wedding night? Did he need a refresher on the birds and bees? The shit was constant; Peeps loved it and gave back as best he could. Peeps, Terry, and Greg agreed to go downtown in a limo and have a great steak dinner for his bachelor party; everyone knew that Terry was assigned to watch Peeps' drinking at the rehearsal dinner and the wedding. Christy gave her first of many sobriety lectures so that everyone knew his role and what behavior was expected. Peeps sat there meekly and accepted the lecture which he knew was long overdue. Terry smiled throughout the lecture, enjoying immensely Peeps' misery—even chiming in here and there just to make matters worse.

The rehearsal dinner was small, quaint, and enormously pleasant; the small group seemed comfortable with each other, sharing their experiences with Christy or Peeps. Some very funny stories were told, mostly at Peeps' expense. He took it good naturedly, he had no choice. Since the wedding was at three, everyone agreed to meet at St. Gertrude at two-thirty. Christy wouldn't be seen until the very last minute, as was the custom. At three o'clock everyone was in place except for Ralphy. Peeps stood in the sanctuary watching the heavy wooden doors; Christy was pacing furiously behind them, her attendants in tow. The priest was waiting, the guests were seated, the men were on the altar, the singer and accompanist in place—all waiting for Ralphy. Finally, Terry volunteered to walk her up the aisle and went to the back of the church to get the wedding started. In walked Ralphy who was immediately cornered by his sister, jabbing him in the chest, hissing curses and blasphemies that any truck driver could only admire. Within seconds brother and sister walked the length of the church to Peeps' waiting arms. The wedding was over in fifteen minutes and the next hour was spent in picture-taking and congratulations from their friends.

The reception was a blast; a very happy and enjoyable group of people celebrating the last of the neighborhood's Irish bachelors—or a gay guy, as some suggested. Maybe he was a gay, old Irish bachelor—that covered all the essential points. Peeps was actually married; the friends around him could not believe it. The next thing phones would be used as cameras. What were the chances of that? Terry and Greg took shifts following Peeps and pouring out more drinks than he actually consumed. He was so bloody happy he did not care what they were doing. He danced and danced, in his very white middle-aged way, dozens of times with Christy. She loved it, he loved it, the photographer loved it and the guests loved it. At eleven, the reception officially ended and a group decided to go the Bubble to party on; Peeps enthusiastically wanted to join in the fun but Christy quietly reminded him that they were leaving mid-morning for Canada and it was time to go home. Besides, it was their wedding night.

They were both buck naked, clothes everywhere, lying in bed and reading cards and counting cash from the many gift givers. Everyone knew that they did not need a new blender or a set of dishes; while a few sent unusual gifts, like a silver frame for their wedding photo, most offered checks to help pay for the wedding expenses. Slowly they were fading, so they hid everything under the mattress and fell into the sleep of death. The alarm was so shrill that Peeps almost threw it against the wall—except he had just painted it. They had to hustle to finish last minute items to be packed and get to the airport. Larry from next door was waiting patiently to get them to American Airlines in time. They were like kids; this was the first time either of them would be on a plane. They did not care about the interminable security wait—you would think they were flying to Moscow. The fact that the flight was an hour late did not deter their excitement. A bucket of cold piss dumped on them would not have changed their mood. The flight to Montreal was horrible; the turbulence was so bad both thought they would be sick. They got off the plane and went to the nearest bar for relief.

Since they had no agenda for their honeymoon, nothing could really get screwed up. The Ritz-Charlton Montreal was old, elegant, and expensive. They could care less. They had only one item on their itinerary, the train to Quebec City and back on Thursday. They had read all of the guidebooks they could find and had a huge list of sights to visit. Peeps spent hours reading to Christy and describing the pictures in the books; he hoped she could share as far as possible the glory of this great French-Canadian city. They took their time as they went from cathedrals to libraries, to museums and plazas to the magnificent public buildings, which were everywhere. Peeps was hoarse by the end of the day from reading placards, legends, signs, and anything written as well as trying to give an adequate description of what was to be seen. He was doing fine until they went to some of the art museums and there he faltered horribly. How do you describe an abstract in orange and red to someone who had never seen color before? He did his best.

The train to and from Quebec City was a marvel, as though time had moved back to nineteen hundred. First class was opulent and they were served a breakfast of bacon, eggs, fruit, hot rolls, coffee, juice and more, if they wanted it. There were only about a dozen passengers, most engrossed in their comput-ers or reading *The Wall Street Journal.* The scenery flew by and the ride was so smooth, it was hard to stay awake. Because it was raining and they only had a few hours before the return train, they hired a car to take them around the city with a very knowledgeable docent to reveal the secrets of Quebec City. He described everything in as much detail as he could and here and there they got out of the car to visit a church or spend a few minutes in a museum. Throughout the trip, Peeps got hooked on the first-class accommodations and the personal service—all with a cost, of course. He wondered what the poor people were doing these days. He had become an instant snob.

With dread they got onto the return flight, although the wait through security was short. The plane left on time; now if it would only stay in the air until O'Hare airport. Christy, now feeling like a seasoned world traveler, fell asleep on his shoulder. For his part, he listened for any change of engine hum or a creak or other unusual noises, ready to pop right up and get off at a second's notice, the only problem was the thirty thousand feet of air between the plane and the ground. What a dick head he was; this was not the Broadway bus where you could get off at every corner. He looked forward to Sunday; they had a day off before going to work and he could veg out watching the promising Chicago Bears play the very good Green Bay Packers in between loads of washing. Neither of them looked forward to Monday, always a shitty day at best but made worse after coming back to reality from a very nice honeymoon. What could happen in a week?

Peeps had been buying from a local organic farmer in western Michigan, outside Grand Rapids. He had built the program so well that when something went wrong there were many customer complaints. The Vale All Natural Farms planted two hundred acres of tomatoes, peppers, green onions and dozens of varieties of leaf lettuce and herbs. They also had a huge greenhouse to grow tomatoes and herbs hydroponically throughout the year, no matter the weather. The weekend shipment failed to show up and no one knew where it was. John Vale swore that it had been shipped and everyone went after the shipper who was bribed by a Whole Foods' manager to leave the entire load at his store and skip Dominick's. No one could prove that money had changed hands, the driver simply said it was a mistake. My bad! Peeps had promoted this new regional source of fresh vegetables and herbs for months, and customers were used to finding the goods front and center. Terry bitched at him; the assistant bitched at him; he got two nasty phone messages from home office and there were at least fifty customer bitches in his email. Christy got off lightly; she was groped on the Red Line and in the process her phone went right out the open door at Fullerton with the groper. Not a single person asked how their honeymoon was. They just wanted their goddamn tomatoes.

Peeps was intrigued and on Tuesday called John Vale about his business. Vale had just begun to dig the eight-foot-deep ditch to hold his second all-season greenhouse. He could sell everything he sold, especially in the middle of the winter. He told Peeps about the basics of his business; most of the greenhouse was below ground, only the continuous skylight was exposed. They had two deep wells on the farm to support the hydroponic growing system; he even had a beehive to pollinate plants; an automatic climate control system ensured that the cute little tomatoes were happy as a clam. They had a koi pond to filter water and keep the algae down. They used a combination of wind machines and solar panels to produce power. In the vast majority of months, they sold back nearly five hundred dollars of energy to the local utility. Would Peeps like to come for a visit and tour the operation—yes, Peeps would like that very much. They agreed on Sunday; Christy declined, saying simply that she did not want to go for a long drive for something she just was not interested in. Peeps was up at dawn for the four-hour trip and came home early evening absolutely fascinated by the entire operation. John and Peeps got along very well, and John talked about needing a partner who had cash to invest. Peeps could be that person and he had the money. But there was a lot to consider. After all, he did not know this man from Adam.

Back to family realities; his Sister called to say that they received a copy of the police report about their missing son. It was two pages long, of which one was a standard fact sheet including name, address, physical description, and similar matters. The last entry in the file was two days after a missing person report was placed. Absolutely nothing, not a fucking thing has been done or even investigated. They did not call friends or the school or anyone he might know. Between a sobbing sister and a growing headache, Peeps was absolutely furious. No wonder they did not want to send the file. It was a folder filled with nothing. Peeps promised to call back if he could think of anything to do. What an odd family: One brother and one nephew gone without a trace. Was there a gene for going missing? He was beginning to think so.

Peeps was finding the work at Dominick's physically harder as the years went on; knees and feet ached every night. Christy often came home to find him packed in ice; the swelling was obvious and no matter how he tried to adjust his work activities, he could not avoid long hours on the hard cement floor of the store. He was well beyond the point of doing the heavy lifting, making the younger people take up that load. He could not figure out how what's his name—his old boss—managed to work to seventy. The guy must have been made of steel. For this reason, and others, he was increasingly interested in a partnership with Vale and his little farm. As they discussed it, Peeps would take over much of the administration and more importantly handle sales. One of their first projects would be to set up a website to tell the world their story. Peeps did not have the skills to do this, so he would have to search very carefully for a group that could both create a site and maintain it so it was fresh and timely. These were just some of the ideas the two men discussed. Peeps had already talked to Bill Barnett and his brother-in-law about his plan for a partnership. Bill was the first to point out that he would probably lose his job once the company found out that he had a side business which would clearly be seen as a conflict of interest. He might be able to work for years before anything came out; he might be found out in a week. Such were the risks. Peeps would be careful and document everything that might be seen as a conflict of interest. No hard sell to his brother produce managers, just glowing reports with his own store.

Ralphy, god bless him, focused on the minutiae—he wanted to see every document, bank statement, loan agreement, tax return, business plan and quarterly statement prepared for the bankers. He would hire people to check the background of this guy and make sure that the deal was for real. He also helped Peeps with a spreadsheet of his own projections of what the company might do in the next two or three years; they had Vale's five-year business plan, but thought they ought to do their own, one that was less optimistic that Vale's version. Where John's view saw profits in the first year, Ralphy saw a break even at the very best—every sprig of rosemary would have to sell at top price. Now Peeps had to have a serious conversation with Christy; she, of course, was following events and had talked to her brother privately to get his sense of this deal. She was not against it; she wanted to make sure that they did not lose a fortune and Peeps' job, which would be very difficult to replace because of his age.

They were still newlyweds and Christy was beginning to feel neglected since the business investment plans got into high gear; Peeps in the evening was meeting with Bill or Ralphy or both, working on the spreadsheet or talking about the deal and what it might mean. They were married for only four months; she did not marry a spreadsheet—the hell with that and she told Peeps so in no uncertain terms. After a bit of an argument, Peeps got the car out and they went to Calo's for a nice quiet dinner and little bedroom romp after. He made plans to have no plans on Sundays for the duration; they would do whatever Christy wanted, even if that was to stay home and watch—listen—to sports.

Christy had become quite a Cubs and Bears fan, much to Peeps' delight; she wanted nothing to do with basketball or hockey—two for four was not bad, Peeps thought. Christy had become quite a Scrabble fan and wanted Peeps to learn the game; she found a set in braille on Amazon and proceeded to beat the shit out of Peeps just about every game. He won one game in their first twenty matches. Even with the disadvantage of not being able to see the whole board— she had to constantly reread each tile and memorize the words played, she was awfully good. Perhaps Peeps was a terrible player. He countered by buying a book on the best words for Scrabble; she found a braille version. Touché.

Peeps got to the point that contracts were prepared and approved by the lawyers; a revised business plan was worked out, one not so optimistic with lots of money set aside for equipment failure and lost revenues because of weather— the outdoor acreage represented more than half of the expected revenue and a wet spring or drought in July would really hurt revenue. Peeps went over and read aloud every page of every document over a two-week period. Christy wrote notes, asked questions and talked to her employer about transferring health insurance to her work rather than Peeps; they absolutely had to be covered, no matter what happened. Both John and Peeps applied for and were accepted for key man life and disability insurance which would go to the company if anything happened to either of them. Because of Peeps' age, his was expensive but the company would cover the premiums.

Peeps had four sets of documents, contract and sales agreement included, stacked on his desk. The lawyers were in, Christy gave the go ahead; John was enthusiastic. What could go wrong? That Thursday Christy got a call from Terry at the store; she missed the call and did not get back to him for an hour.

CHAPTER TEN:
A Change of Plans

On Thursdays and Mondays a huge trailer truck would show up at the dock with merchandise to stock the store for three days. Getting everything off and in the right place in the store was a bit of an art. Inventory should be placed as close as possible to where it was sold without inconveniencing customers; it was not easy and they used a plan-o-gram, a store map, where every numbered pallet would go before the kids and the night crew would begin stocking shelves. The operation was always organized chaos with one of the assistant store managers leading the charge. All the pallets came through the produce department; the dock was right behind it. The kids would always fight over who would run the folk lifts; the assistant manager did not care, but it always drove Peeps crazy. The college kids should run the show, not the high school brats.

This Thursday was a real mess; it was both sleeting and snowing at the same time; the wind blew the mess onto the dock and into the back room of the produce department. One kid spent the entire evening doing nothing but shoveling the mess from the dock. The dock was so slippery that a load almost went over the side, forklift, kid and all. Trying to go forward, the lift just kept sliding toward the end of the dock. The kid did the right thing and simply stopped instead of trying to make a correction. The assistant manager took over and got the load into the store. Peeps kept yelling at the kids to keep the floor within the store dry; two dry mops and a wringer were used; of course the kids did not listen and failed to do their job. They were preoccupied with their turn to drive the forklift. Everyone kept slipping on the wet floor and Peeps kept yelling about the floor. It did no good; the kids were clueless so Peeps took over the mopping and in the process slipped just as a loaded forklift was headed for him. It ran over his left ankle and the stupid kid panicked and backed up and over the ankle a second time. Peeps was screaming in agony, writhing in pain so excruciating he pissed himself and nearly passed out. Everyone froze in place; after an eternity, someone called 911.

He was taken to St. Francis in Evanston, as that was the closest hospital; he really wanted to go to Evanston Hospital where he could engage the services of Illinois Bone and Joint Clinic and the world-famous Dr. Stephen Haddad, one of the greatest specialists in ankle surgery and replacements. It took four hours for the staff at St. Francis to stabilize him; they gave him the equivalent of a horse tranquilizer to get him some relief. Terry still had not heard from Christy so he called Greg next door to let her know what had happened to Peeps. Greg found Christy just walking into the door and offered to drive her to the hospital. Christy, sat down for five minutes before leaving and sobbed; she cried for Peeps, for his business plans and for herself. How would she care for him? She could barely take care of herself. On the way to the hospital, she called Barnett and asked him to talk to John and tell him there would be an indefinite postponement of their plans. John was secretly furious and cursed like a mad man for an hour. He had already made some commitments pending Peeps' investment. He could be in real financial trouble if he could not work out his commitments.

Christy came into the hospital room and immediately tripped over a chair, landing on Peeps who cried out in agony. She did everything she could to comfort him, eventually settling on a corner of the bed simply holding his hand. Nothing would happen tonight, so after an hour or so, they all left. She told Peeps that she would meet him at Evanston once he was moved. It took hours to arrange the transfer the next day and all St. Francis could do was keep him sedated and keep the ankle compressed. Once at Evanston, the entire rest of the day was spent on x-rays and scans. Various doctors came and went, each interested in his general health, ordering blood tests and a chest x-ray. He was deemed fit to die. Christy came in late in the afternoon and the two of them talked and cried over the mess he had become. Barnett showed up at the end of the day with a raft of papers to sign: Peeps was applying for disability which would pay him for the rest of his life plus he would sue his employer for unsafe working conditions, demanding a substantial lump sum payment. Peeps balked; he would never be able to go back to his old job. Christy and Bill had talked to the doctors from the Bone and Joint Institute—Peeps would be lucky to keep his foot. Working as he did in the past was highly unlikely. The two explained this as carefully as they could but Peeps just went into a huge funk. Christy made him sign the papers nevertheless.

Haddad and his physician assistant came to his room on day three to talk turkey about what could and could not happen. They felt that they might save the ankle, but it would take several surgeries and many months of physical therapy to get him up and walking. There were no promises as to how well he would walk and at what level of pain. They described in detail what was injured and what they could do to correct the ankle. They were kind and patient and answered every question he had. There was nothing they could do until the swelling went down, so surgery was scheduled for the middle of next week. Peeps now had nothing to do but watch television and reflect on his situation: newly married to a lovely and wonderful woman, ready to sign an agreement that might have set them up for life, a working guy who actually had money in the bank and a paid-up house. As he brooded, he got more and more pissed at the store assistant who managed the stock transfer that afternoon and the stupid kids and their obsession with driving the forklift. By the time Christy came to visit, he was in a black mood which even she could not coax him out of.

The week before surgery was a crawl; hospital routine set in. Eating meals, getting cleaned up, sitting in a chair, learning to use crutches to move three feet, going to the bathroom; each involved substantial discomfort which he got used to. Christy was losing weight and Peeps had a talk with her about eating more and that she did not have to come to the hospital every night. They did agree that she would take Uber home instead of the Purple Line to the Red Line to Granville station. Peeps was not eating much, but Christy took to the hospital food like it was homemade. She would finish what he had not eaten. What Peeps wanted most was a martini and his friend and neighbor Larry took care of that on occasion: martinis from a thermos. Very elegant. They were ice cold and they did the trick. Christy caught them red-handed and exploded saying he was jeopardizing his health. Peeps said that there was no evidence of that, and she knew it. She apologized for overreacting and actually became a conspirator; on the weekend when she came to visit, she would bring a thermos.

Thursday came bright and early—no organization started the work day as early as a hospital, something Peeps could not understand. Why is six thirty the magic time for surgery? All Peeps could remember, which was a good thing, was that the operating room was like a meat locker—he could not get enough blankets to keep warm. He was given a shot of a very nice drug to help him relax; it was better than gin. He wondered if he could get some on the outside. Surgical nurses worked like beavers to prepare his ankle, leg, and foot. After what seemed like an age, he was anesthetized and sent to happy land while the gremlins went to work on him. Christy was there to meet him in the recovery room and he was never so happy to see her in his life. Haddad reported that the operation went as well as expected, but that at least one further surgery would have to happen before they knew the outcome for sure. Peeps hardly heard any of this and Christy realized that he needed time before they talked further.

The next week was pain and gloom; Peeps was again suffering from mild depression and meds were ordered to help. Visitors came and went and flowers filled the room, to the point of being ridiculous. Peeps would have preferred bottles of Tanqueray. They took up less space and had real medicinal value. One visitor was Bill Barnett to talk business. Together with Christy, he had applied for long-term disability insurance on Peeps' behalf; that was an automatic so Peeps signed the forms and that was that. Bill estimated that he would receive about sixty percent of his base salary for the rest of his life. He would not be rich, but it would certainly cover the bills. Next he brought up the issue of suing Dominick's for substantial money damages. This alarmed Peeps—he was a loyal employee and just was not sure if a lawsuit was right or appropriate. Bill talked him through the issues calmly and logically; the company had a moral and legal obligation to keep a safe workplace. They had failed to do so and as a result had ruined Peeps' life—they needed to pay for their negligence. He further explained that he was not trained for this kind of lawsuit and they would have to hire specialists. Bill wanted only the best and had an agreement with Stein, Hall, Douglas, LLC to handle the case; they would take thirty percent as their retainer, assuming they won. If they did not win, Peeps would not be responsible for any legal bills.

The trial lawyers on television seemed ready to sue the Pope if they could make a buck; Peeps did not want to be associated with that crowd. Bill explained Stein, Hall was a first-class operation, and turned down ninety percent of the litigants who came to them. They only took cases that had substantial merit and that they were sure they could win. They would demand two million dollars from Dominick's, for lost wages but more importantly for pain, suffering, and loss of lifestyle. Peeps was shocked by the amount; he called Christy, but found out that Bill had talked to her first and she was in complete agreement that he should sue. He carefully read Bill's documents with him and with Stein, Hall. He signed everything and thanked Bill for his help; he also marveled how quickly Bill moved right along. Bill was sharp and aggressive, and he would go a long way in his young career.

As the days passed fewer and fewer visitors came by; it was both understandable and a relief. There was only so much chit chat and bullshit to go around. Telling the same stories six times became tedious and he was suddenly very self-conscious about his injuries. He felt odd, different from everyone else. No one could possibly understand how he felt and what a downer this whole mess was. He was anxious about the future and his marriage; would Christy still love him? Could they resume their young marriage as they had before? Would he be able to walk or be a cripple for the rest of his life? How would he fill his days if he were not working? He felt like he was being buried under an avalanche of huge boulders, one piling on after the other with vicious regularity. He talked to Christy about some of this and she did her best to reassure him. She would not leave him; he had married her even though she was handicapped, why should she not follow suit? Their talks helped and the meds were better yet.

Terry called in the morning and asked if Peeps would like company and a sandwich and a fruit smoothie for lunch. Peeps was delighted to hear from Terry and readily cancelled his hospital lunch. When Terry arrived he seemed subdued and said little; they ate lunch in complete silence. Peeps thought that there might be a problem at home and Terry needed someone to talk to, so he broke the silence and asked about home life. Terry said under the circumstances, everything was going very well. His wife clearly recognized that he had been caught off guard and the young man absolutely tried to seduce him, not the other way around. They talked about the store for a bit and what was going on at Dominick's in general; Terry had the impression that all the new stores like Aldi and Trader Joe's were making life miserable for traditional chain stores.

Just as quickly, Terry changed subjects and got to his real reason for coming—senior management wanted Terry to talk Peeps out of suing the company. Peeps said nothing while Terry went through his presentation, clearly well prepared with legal advice from Dominick's home office. If they could get the lawyers out of it, Dominick's was prepared to pay him one hundred thousand dollars in a lump sum with the agreement that Peeps would drop the lawsuit. His main point was that the company had been a good employer and had advanced Peeps quickly as a young man. He owed the company, his company. Peeps thought a minute and simply shook his head no and said he could not do that. Terry explained, almost whined that he was under tremendous pressure to get Peeps to change his mind. As a friend, could he not find a way to accept some kind of arrangement other than the outrageous two million dollars in damages?

Peeps said nothing. Terry started to leave and actually told him he did not blame him; he would have sued if he were in Peeps' shoes. He told him that this was not going to ruin their friendship; he just had to ask. Peeps said he understood. Before leaving, he had one more thing to tell Peeps. The kid that had run over Peeps, Toby, who was a junior at Lane Tech—one of the selective Chicago high schools—had committed suicide. His parents had not seen him around the house on Saturday afternoon. His mother had gone to the basement to do laundry and found him hanging from a water pipe. The boy was quiet and a bit of a loner so his parents thought a part time job would do him good, help him come out of himself. And it was working; he made friends at Dominick's and joined the gang for burgers on the weekend after their shifts. Peeps was crushed; he did not even know the boy because Toby worked in general grocery and had only been there for a few months. He put his head in his pillow and cried like a baby as Terry patted his back to comfort him on his way out the door.

A week of absolutely nothing to do except Let's Make a Deal and the Price is Right. Peeps admitted to himself that he was hooked on both shows. He managed to make sure that physical or occupational therapy would not take place between nine and eleven. They had yet to cast the foot, waiting to pull drains; until they did, the therapy went on until he collapsed—and that was only one half hour. He was surprised how little strength he had. Everything was a chore; he worked the crutches twice a day and learned how to use a three-wheeled scooter that supported his wounded leg; he used his right leg for motion. It was rather fun once you got the hang of it and it was sure better than crutches. Once he was stabilized, he would go to a rehab center for four weeks before the next surgery. But first the swelling had to go down so they could put on a cast.

Cast finally on, Peeps and his three-wheeler moved to a rehab facility called Symphony in Evanston; the place was nothing exceptional, the usual institutional joint, not too different than the hospital but without the hustle and bustle. Again, he had rehab twice a day but he could not protect his special times for his TV shows, no matter how hard he tried. Everything he did had to protect his ankle, which meant no weight-bearing activities. They used weights to build up arm and shoulder strength, the usual routine on crutches, although he did not know why since he had his little green cart to get himself around. The location made it more difficult for Christy; she had to Uber until she found out that there was a Purple line stop just two blocks away. Peeps insisted that she Uber at night. They spent a lot of time talking about how lonely she was without Peeps around the house. The friends were great, continuing to be supportive, visiting and inviting her for dinner on the weekend. She was grateful but her sense of loneliness could not be overcome so easily; she and Peeps were real emotional losers.

Surgery time came before he knew it; it was both a relief and a real source of additional anxiety. What happened if the doctor could not work his magic? Would more surgery be needed? How long would this circus go on? Could his marriage survive? No matter what, his life would never be the same. In the meantime, the lawyers were hard at it. Peeps was deposed for three hours; Terry was there during the meeting as were the store lawyers who did everything they could to confuse the events of that day. Peeps was not rattled and he was not intimidated; he knew the truth as did everyone else in the room. His lawyers were thorough; they even deposed the truck driver. Everyone in the area when the accident happened was in their net. Terry was required to witness every one of the depositions and report back to corporate. Frankly, they did not trust their own lawyers who assured management that everything was going smoothly. Terry reported just the opposite. Strangely, Terry earned the respect of management for his efforts on behalf of the company. Maybe he would get that larger store after all.

Stein, Hall had already filed suit in civil court; they did not waste a minute. They put intense pressure on management and it was known that factions at corporate had formed, for settlement or going to court. The problem was that the lawyers did not leave them much wiggle room and any settlement would have to include an immediate substantial lump sum payment and a five-year annuity for the rest, purchased from a AAA insurance company. Terry thought that this might be settled quickly; the depositions were so damning that it was hard to see a jury denying the two million, and possibly adding more to the settlement. The assistant store manager was immediately fired after his deposition; he had been on paid leave at half salary. Another life comes crashing down because of gross stupidity, thought Peeps.

The second surgery was much quicker and he was in and out in two hours; he was back to drains, catheter and IV. The report from the doctor was not enthusiastic; the surgery was successful, but much depended on how well he healed and physical therapy. He got the lecture multiple times a day from the physician's assistant, the nurses, Christy, and the cleaning lady that he had to give everything to his therapy post-surgery. Back to the rehab center and back to the routine of transferring from the scooter to a chair, to a shower bench, to standing up on one leg and getting in and out of bed by himself. Christy had decided that she would take four months of family leave to help Peeps in his transition home. She worked with the social worker to prepare the house, from a chair lift for the front steps to getting the right equipment for his bathroom. Bob Cox came to the rescue once again and made all the physical changes needed. In three and one-half weeks a driver brought him home to the love and care of the beautiful Christy. His first day out, he went for a martini at the Bubble to say hello to his Mates who had been nothing but kind the last three months.

They settled in as a couple better than each thought; after a week or so, it was time to test the effectiveness of those little blue pills. Peeps crossed his fingers and prayed for the best. He hoped he was not the monkey fucking a basketball. Dr. Frank told him that if these did not work, there were several other choices which were usually successful. Joy in Mudville, the first night went just fine. It was though each had to relearn about the other, what they liked and how they should prepare for sex. Peeps was nervous as hell and he was certain Christy was anxious. They talked about nothing but how they were going to spend the rest of their lives. They both decided that this traveling business had much merit; Peeps would start driving soon and that would give them lots of options on how to spend their time while Christy was on leave. They even talked about Christy not going back to work, although health insurance was a major issue. Besides, she explained, she liked work and felt a real need to continue to help people who could not help themselves. They also talked about John and his farm; Peeps had not heard from him, simply because Bill and Christy had taken all of his calls. They agreed that the contracts would sit on the desk unsigned until he knew more about his ability to work. The program would not work unless Peeps could manage the back office and do the selling and marketing.

The reason Peeps never heard from John was because Bill and Christy blocked John's number on Peeps' phone. But John had called, mostly Bill but often enough with Christy; he was really upset. Each call with Bill was more strident and demanding; where was the goddamn contract and money; they had a deal and John was in terrible financial straits. The calls got uglier and Bill finally had to hang up; he blocked John's number as well. He asked Christy to do the same. John, it seems, anticipating a cash infusion had gone ahead and signed a contract with a builder to start on the second greenhouse, this in the absence of a contract and a check. John was so sure of the deal that he jumped the gun. If he did not start now, he reasoned, he would not be able to start until spring. There was not much building and concrete work done in Western Michigan over winter. Further, sales were down because of poor growing conditions for the traditional crops he planted each year that made up the bulk of his income. The three talked about this and could not believe what he had done; they were certainly sorry for his crop failure and his stupidity.

Stein, Hall had been silent for months, but that surprised no one. But they got a call four months later that their partner, Gilmour Drummond, would like to meet with Christy, Peeps and Bill. Not knowing what to expect, the trio traveled downtown to the AT&T building for a face to face with Drummond. What they found was a middle-aged man, obviously from the UK at some point, with wild hair, messy suit and tie and an amiable smile which was totally misleading.

Drummond was called the Snake behind his back; he would do everything except shoot the Pope on the high altar to win—and he might reconsider on the Pope at that. In thirty years of civil litigation, he had lost only two cases when he was a young lawyer. He made it a point of pride not to repeat those two follies anytime soon.

Mr. Snake's assistant served coffee and small cakes on bone china so thin you could see through it. Peeps guessed that the china was several thousand a place setting. Courtesies were extended to Peeps on his troubles and what a beautiful and charming woman Christy must be. The small talk went on for one-half hour, covering everything from the new season at the opera to the future of his favorite baseball team, the Chicago White Sox. None of the three contributed much, except the usual yes, no, and how fascinating. When Drummond started talking about his love for Chicago, Peeps joined in and told of his own plans to study and research the early history of the city. That seemed to interest the Snake very much. Meanwhile, Peeps' ankle was killing him and he really wanted to get this meeting going; further he wanted to know what the fuck was happening with the lawsuit. He was dying of curiosity and the Snake knew it. Finally down to business just after a pain pill.

Drummond reported that they had the company on the ropes. Peeps told of the informal offering of one hundred thousand, which made the Snake smile. The company had offered one million dollars, all in an annuity over ten years. Naturally that was rejected outright, Drummond told them; it was not even worth bothering them with such a trifle. The firm countered with the two million, half in cash and half payable over seven years. Drummond felt that this was significant progress, but wanted his client's opinion on how much to concede in the negotiations. Bill felt strongly that they should not move from their position. Peeps quietly reminded both litigators that there was the matter of attorney fees and that a lesser settlement would greatly reduce what he and Christy received. The Snake again smiled. Drummond proposed to Bill as much as Peeps that they separate their fees from the compensation due the McAvoys. He proposed that they offer Dominick's a settlement of one and one half million; half paid out in cash and the other half paid through a seven-year annuity purchased from a highly rated insurance company and controlled by his firm. He and Bill would haggle about fees separately. Both deals would be signed by all parties to the suit so that Peeps had assurance that he was not liable for a huge legal bill. After some conversation, they decided that this would be their final offer, otherwise they would go to civil court.

Terry started bringing lunch once a week; he was only three blocks from the house. They enjoyed these visits and Terry found the time as a release from the pressure at home and at the store. He told Peeps straight out that he missed him as produce manager; that department alone now counted for twenty percent of store sales. The problem was the current manager just did not have the imagination to take hold of the growing demand for healthy and fresh eating, which meant vegetables and fruits. This area and prepared food should fuel steady increases in store revenue and profits; unfortunately, his store was down three percent versus last year and he did not see the trend changing. Aldi had moved in two blocks north and that did not help matters. Dominick's was a privately held company and so financial results were not made readily available. The old man who founded the company was sick and was sure to retire soon. The grapevine buzzed with rumors that the company had lost money the last two years. He urged Peeps to settle with the company just in case.

Naturally, Peeps called Bill immediately, and when he called back he told him about the conversation with Terry. If the company filed for bankruptcy or just closed down, he would be out of luck. Bill went to work and three days later they had an agreement for one million, two hundred and fifty thousand with the lawyers to be paid three hundred thousand. It was signed, sealed, and delivered within a day. Four days later Peeps received a check in the mail for seven hundred thousand dollars and annuity contract for the rest payable over seven years; as a result they would receive a monthly stipend through the end of year seven. They were overwhelmed and extremely grateful; the only problem was the money would do nothing to improve his health and give him his life back. They agreed to tell no one about the settlement except Ralphy. In particular, Peeps would be very careful when he went to the Bubble. If asked what was going on, he would simply say that there was no progress in the negotiations. Eventually, it would blow over as old news.

They invited Ralphy for dinner at Gene and Georgetti's, the evening on them, of course. He was delighted to accompany them and made the reservations to ensure a first floor sitting. They got dressed up and hired a limo to take them to dinner and back. After small talk, Ralphy was delighted to hear the good news. They talked in earnest over drinks about what should be done with the money. Ralphy insisted that nothing should go to John to bail him out; they had no obligation to him. He acted prematurely and that was entirely his doing. Peeps told Ralphy about his municipal bond fund which reinvested dividends each month; all agreed that a large portion of the money would go into this fund. It would grow tax free over the years. The one major expenditure which Peeps thought was needed was a systematic overhaul of the house, especially the kitchen and one of the bathrooms. The exterior needed painting and new windows were long overdue. Christy agreed that she would call Bob Cox tomorrow morning.

A visiting nurse came to the house every day as well as a physical therapist. Both would end soon as the insurance had limits on these services. Peeps would go for physical therapy in the surgeon's office in Wilmette; the entire first floor was devoted to state-of-the-art equipment and the best certified therapists. With the help of Dick across the street, he practiced getting in and out of his car. Christy folded the cart and put it in the back; she came with him for every session, mostly to manage the cart but to watch progress and make sure Peeps was not slacking off. If she thought he was, he heard about it on the way home. Progress was slow and the pain was terrible, even though he took a Norco before going to PT. After each session, he came home very down; he was sure that this program was doing nothing except make him miserable. Christy left him alone and even encouraged him to roll down to the Bubble for a martini or two—but no more than two, she reminded him, lest he run into something on the way home. God forbid that he should fall.

After four long months, he could see progress and it was decided to take the cast off and fit him with an orthopedic boot. He was told he could walk on his ankle, but to take it easy, especially in the beginning. Under no circumstances should he walk without the boot. In fact, the boot would probably be a permanent addition to his wardrobe. The nurse assured him they were very fashionable, his choice of black or battleship gray. Peeps walked out of the doctor's office, profusely thanking everyone for their efforts. He had strict instructions to put ice on the ankle every night to keep the swelling and pain down. Nurse Christy, aka Nurse Cratchet, was Johnny on the spot with the ice and the pillow while they listened to television or read in the evenings.

With Peeps directing, Christy took over meals while she was home. Everything in the refrigerator had its place; she identified items by their shape of the container or the smell of its contents. Peeps had learned long ago to make sure that the entire house would cause no surprises for Christy. Once she was back to work, Peeps took over as chef de cuisine. He also drove her each morning; she begged off on the evening ride as she was never quite sure when she would be home. Christy going back to work was a huge adjustment for Peeps; he watched some TV, including his two favorite game shows in the morning. He devoured the newspaper, often throwing it across the room in disgust. He cleaned something every day—dust here and vacuum there. It was not enough; he did not really have a purpose or function until he got a phone call from the Snake asking if he was intruding. No, not exactly, thought Peeps. Could they meet at the Union League Club for lunch next week?

CHAPTER ELEVEN:

The Man with a Plan

Peeps called the Club to inquire about proper dress; he was told that a tie was not necessary but a jacket was. He wore both so as not to stand out; the suit was brand new and the most money he ever spent on clothes. When he arrived, he was shown to a private dining room where Drummond was already waiting; he was a bit late and apologized. The Uber car did not show for ten minutes; the Snake waved it off and offered him a drink. Peeps had a Guinness while Gilmour—they were now on a first name basis—ordered white wine. Menus were presented and Gilmour made several suggestions. While waiting for food, they got down to business. Drummond was ready to retire in two years; the firm had a mandatory retirement age. While obviously not from Chicago, he had fallen in love with the city when he came to the University of Chicago for a semester. He wanted to write the definitive book about Chicago, its history, and its culture.

He needed a researcher and he was interested in Peeps' plans about his research. He admitted to Gilmour that they were not well formulated, he planned to use the facilities at the Newberry; in fact he had already made trips to the library to see what was what. Drummond proposed a deal whereby he would do the writing and they would share equally the credit as co-authors. At the very least, he would get the University of Chicago Press to publish the book; they could also self-publish through Amazon. In either case, they would use an agent to advise on the best strategy. Gilmour envisioned the book to be easy to read, light with lots of anecdotes and bits of history that readers would find fascinating and intriguing. The last thing he wanted was a dull chronological history of the city from its founding to the present.

He talked on and on about the kinds of material Peeps should look for; readers loved scandal and sex and money. Dig up the dirt, even if it were conjecture. Look for funny and not so funny information—political and gangland feuds, for example. God knows Chicago was filled with this kind of filth. Peeps had finished his lunch and Drummond had only taken a bite or two when Peeps said simply yes. He would be delighted to work on the project. Of course, they would split royalties. They agreed that each topic or person would be a separate Word file; Peeps would provide a general outline of the facts and a series of bullet points to fill in the details. It was essential that if he quoted anything verbatim, he would provide Gilmour the book title, publisher, and other pertinent information. There must be no plagiarism. Gilmour would provide Peeps with a page or two summary about citing sources.

He spent the evening talking with Christy about the book and could think and talk of nothing else. Christy wondered why Peeps did not take the Red Line, drive or take an Uber to the library. The Red Line was too far to walk, there was no parking and Uber would cost sixty dollars a day, at least. He could catch the Broadway Bus in front of the library; there were seats there. Further, he liked the atmosphere of the bus, the odd characters who rode with him; he was not in any hurry. He would spend a couple hours or so each day researching items from the Drummond list. Once a week he would stop at Bob's Burgers for lunch, a new place that received great reviews. The next day he received an email containing a simple agreement between the parties. Printed, signed, and mailed, he now had a reason to get up in the morning.

They agreed to meet at the Club once a month to talk about ideas and subjects Peeps had uncovered. His first presentation to Gilmour was about a disgraced alderman. Searching the internet and old issues of the Chicago Tribune, he found huge amounts of content that included investigations, subpoenas, interviews and commentary. Everyone, it seemed, knew the scam was on but could not figure it out. As agreed, he had prepared a synopsis and factual bullet points for future writing. Gilmour loved the topic but had a few comments which he penned on the pages; it reminded Peeps of Nanna's poisoned red pencil through high school and college. He took the suggestions good-naturedly and agreed that he would provide better content delivery. He needed to practice to meet what Gilmour thought he would need. He spent the weekend reorganizing and rewriting and posted in on their shared Word site. The comments back were few and he was told it was much better. Gilmour explained it was difficult for one person to know exactly what the other wanted and needed. He admitted that he was not even sure himself. But this was the kind of story that would speak to Chicagoans about their city.

As they met each month, they got to know each other; two people could not have been more different from each other. Gilmour was a brahmin from the North Shore with education, sophistication, and money, lots of it. Peeps still acted like a working man, even though he had enough money in the bank to buy Peoria. Gilmour spoke about his failed marriage after almost thirty-five years. His wife, he explained was extremely conservative; when their only son announced that he was gay, she blamed the situation on her husband—he should have spent more time with the boy. Among the many casualties, he was stuck with a two-million-dollar house in Wilmette. Even though the Great Recession was over for several years, real estate prices in the North Shore never recovered. There were hundreds, perhaps many hundreds of houses, over a million dollars and no one wanted them. He hated living in a fourteen-room house by himself, commuting to work by train every day and the dullness of his career and life. Sadly, his wife never spoke to her son; Gilmour kept in touch and went to dinner with his son and his partner weekly. He was not going to lose his son, no matter what anyone thought.

It was clear to Peeps that retirement was going to be sooner rather than later. Gilmour finally found a family to rent the house, completely furnished, for a ridiculous price and he rented a very nice and expensive apartment downtown in the burgeoning West Loop, once the home of butchers and fishmongers, now the place to live and work. He also found out that his son lived in Edgewater, fast becoming the new Boy's Town. At least five of his neighbors were gay couples, almost all having moved in within the last two years. It seemed that a lot of people wanted to live in the neighborhood—good news for long-term homeowners. Gilmour had a sailboat in Monroe Harbor and he and Christy were invited for a day on the lake. There he met the son and his mate as well as someone named Miss Jenny. Peeps had no idea who she was and avoided anything even close to finding out. As it turned out she was very reserved and said little the entire afternoon. Father, son, and boyfriend took over the chores of sailing and he and Christy had a magnificent day. Lathered in sunscreen and wearing floppy hats, they looked like seasoned sea dogs. Christy knew what he was thinking and whispered in his ear that a boat was out of the question. Shit.

Weeks and months passed in their happy routine of work, the library, taking small trips to Wisconsin and Michigan and generally enjoying life. Peeps made sure, with few exceptions, that he was home by about seven in order to make dinner and enjoy time with his wife before she went to bed. Driving her to work in the morning turned out to be a real pain, but she was so appreciative he would never change their routine. Gilmour was happily beavering away on the book; he had settled on the theme of the unwritten history of Chicago. The book would have some forty stories, in chronological order, anecdotal and often very funny. Gilmour had a dry wit and was wonderfully sarcastic; Peeps figured that all those years as a litigator were coming out.

January turned out to be a really shitty month—more than the usual Chicago January. Peeps spent most of his free time using the snow blower to keep the alley and his sidewalk cleared. The work exhausted him and he had to sit down every ten or fifteen minutes because of the throbbing pain in his ankle. He had not been to the library for a week so he searched the internet for stories and ideas. But it just was not the same and he was frustrated and tired of winter. Christy had not gone to work for two days, attempting to work from home with little success. The city systems were so out of date, she kept getting cut off from her work files and databases. She was crabby, he was hurting, and they spent a miserable Friday stuck in the house together. They ordered pizza which neither really wanted but they could not agree on something else. They tried a new place in Rogers Park but were sorely disappointed. Dinner made both crabbier. After three glasses of wine, Christy announced that she wanted to join the Catholic Church. She had been talking to Nancy across the street and she had agreed to be her sponsor. Peeps was stunned; people were leaving the church not joining up. There were more ex-Catholics than practicing members. The priest scandal had raged for years and had no end to it. They quarreled as never before, but her mind was made up, and she expected him to start going to church again with her. Peeps fled to the TV with a very large martini.

Christy spent the spring studying and praying with the expectation that she would be baptized just before Easter. It was a very formal process, known as the Rite of Christian Initiation for Adults, and there were five others taking instruction in the faith. She often asked Peeps questions but he found it diffi- cult to help most of the time; it had been so long and so much had changed, he felt absolutely stupid that he did not know the answers. Fortunately, he was a good internet searcher and came up with many of the answers after the fact. He was now back in the church for life. Christy wanted to know how much they contributed each week, and Peeps said he paid one hundred dollars per month electronically. Christy informed him in no uncertain terms that they would be giving five hundred and he had strict instructions to call the rectory and get the change made forthwith. What could he say; they could afford it and more. He also sent checks to Loyola Academy and the Midwest Jesuits for general support of priests in training. Each received ten thousand dollars, and he got personal phone calls as a thank you. They also wanted to introduce Peeps to Fr. Terry who founded a school, St. Aloysius in Nairobi, Kenya, devoted specifically for children whose parents died from AIDS or lived in the worst slum just outside the capital. And of course, Peeps could not forget the Loyola alumni association, which was so good, if he moved to the moon tomorrow, they would have his new cell number and email address within a week. The place was a real machine and alumni gave generously; it helped that half their students came from the North Shore. Give us a boy and we will give you a man—of God.

Several months after her baptism, Christy had a very strange experience, one that she thought was very spiritual and meaningful. Twice a year, management called for an early meeting, one that began at seven in the morning. Basically, that meant that she had to get up at five in order to be on her way by six. She never asked Peeps to drive as she felt guilty about getting him out of bed so early for such a ridiculous meeting. While on the Red Line to downtown, a woman introduced herself and said that she had seen Christy at St. Gertrude. She also knew that she was newly baptized. Jane explained that she wanted to go back to the church; she had married a divorced man who had recently died. Naturally, she could not take communion while still married, and therefore mostly avoided mass as well. They sat and talked all the way downtown and agreed to meet at church on Sunday and she would introduce her to Father Bill, the pastor. Jane met with the priest after mass and was pronounced an active Catholic. Jane sat with Christy and Peeps every Sunday for church and they became fast friends, often going out together or coming to the McAvoy house for Sunday dinner.

Gilmour reported at their next meeting that he needed at least ten juicy or funny stories to complete the book. But he asked Peeps not to use anything that was less than ten years old. Peeps thought that was a pity as there was no end to the nonsense going on in city government. Alderman seemingly were born to be indicted. Peeps decided to focus on the time just before and after the Chicago fire; his research told of marvelous stories of heroism, kindness, greed, and general chicanery. Nothing brought out the best and the worst in people like a disaster of biblical proportions. The Fire was all that and more. Most of the Tribune files were lost so he had to depend on secondary sources, which Gilmour did not prefer; but he had to live with it. By the end of the summer, his work was done; frankly, as much as he liked the work, he was now tired of going to the library, working for days on his synopses, and talking through each one with Gilmour. They had to finalize a title for the book and locked on to "The History of Chicago: Stories of Heroism and Chicanery".

And then there was Terry. He still came to the house almost every week for lunch and he was more and more depressed and scared about his job and the future of the company. The founder had died and the family had tried to run the company by committee — no one wanted to agree on who should take over. Then came the news that the family wanted to sell, but after six months, there were no takers. The chain had not been profitable for over two years and cash and morale were in very short supply. Peeps urged Terry to bail, but not to another retailer; Peeps pointed to this company called Amazon which started selling books and now sold everything—including food and drinks. Peeps was convinced that Amazon was going to take over the world. Terry looked skeptical, but got his point. Terry would focus on suppliers and consultants to retail; he knew of hundreds of companies with whom he had been doing business and had direct contacts he could call and network.

Peeps hung around the house for two or three weeks without a plan. Suddenly he realized his tenth wedding anniversary was months away and they should do something special. How about a trip to Paris, perhaps a river cruise down the Seine. That would be just the ticket. Ralphy was coming for a duck dinner on Sunday—Peeps' specialty. He would ask him; he had traveled extensively. Peeps could not wait for Christy to come home to talk about the trip. She barely got into the door when he proposed the idea; they would take ten days and see Paris and sail the Seine. Christy was delighted and he spent the evening searching prices from different airlines. They would go in October when it was a bit cooler and the crowds were smaller. Peeps also learned that he could pre-arrange tickets for all the major sights like the Louvre.

While the ducks were happily roasting away, Peeps and Christy talked about their plans. Peeps started off with his research on coach tickets. This brought out an uproarious laugh from Ralphy; he asked if Peeps was really going to put his sister in the back of the plane? Perhaps Peeps was suddenly poor? Did the bond fund stop paying his eight thousand dollars a month tax free? Christy chimed in: Perhaps she could get a part time job on the weekend to help pay for the trip? Ralphy: Peeps could dress in his worst clothes and beg for money on the streets. Maybe a car title loan on his SUV would be the answer to his poverty? And so it went for a good five minutes. Peeps turned red, then got seriously pissed, and finally laughed at his own folly. Ralphy checked his phone for a travel agent who handled people with money. Her name was Zava something; no one ever called her anything but Zava. Raphy also reminded them that they would both need special arrangements if they were going to get around. Christy could walk, Peeps could not. Ralphy ate nearly an entire duck, with noodles and gravy plus salad. Peeps was surprised he was still alive.

They met Zava at her business, a very swanky office in a new office tower on Goose Island. Peeps checked for his wallet, watch, money clip and his testicles, sure they would all be gone by the time with meeting was over. She explained that she only took clients of a certain class and agreed to see them as a favor to Ralphy. After proper introductions, they got down to business. She was told that there was no budget, just the kind of clients she loved. She also knew of their various physical limitations. She assured them that nothing would be a problem. They would have a docent/driver who would have an electric scooter in the car for Peeps. They would stay at the Four Seasons Hotel George V, one of the best in Paris. It came to the staggering price of fifteen hundred dollars a night plus value added tax. But who was counting, certainly not Zava. She arranged entry passes for all the major sights, making sure that they would take at least two day trips out of Paris; she made reservations at all of the best restaurants. Peeps called the banker at Chase to make sure that their credit card limits would be the highest possible. He would load up on euros once in France. He would need all of it.

Next, they went shopping for clothes and spent a fortune. He helped Christy as best he could, but the sales lady at Nordstrom's did the heavy lifting. They each had plenty of casual clothes for the day, so the focus was on what to wear for the evening. Peeps would always need a jacket, tie optional. Zava even spent time going over menus; she was impressed that Peeps could read and speak some French. He had been studying online for the last three weeks. Christy found travel books in braille and she spent the evenings reading up on everything possible they might need. Peeps did the same, but online. They compared notes so that they were both in agreement as to how to act properly. Ralphy checked in regularly to see how they were coming along. He gave them an A+ for their efforts. Take off was a week away, and they were as excited as kids at Christmas.

The trip was a resounding success; they had a blast and Peeps absolutely refused to add up the damage. He finally got over the fact that he no longer was a working guy at Dominick's but someone with resources he could never have imagined. Everyone knew that they were going to France, they even knew that they were using a travel agent to make arrangements for getting around. On a stack of bibles, they swore Ralphy and themselves to complete secrecy about what they spent, where they stayed, and what restaurants they visited. They did not want family and friends to even suspect how much money they earned. Friendships and relationships would never be the same if others knew of the grand plan. Their driver, also their docent, was so good that Christy missed nothing; he took the time to find information in braille for her which she could read in the car between destinations. They had to text Zava about how much to tip him. They talked between themselves about the trip for months. They never tired of it; it was just so great.

They were seeing more and more of The Sister, although usually by herself; her husband did not care to join her and her kids were in high school and college and had no interest in visiting with an uncle they hardly spoke to. If they only knew, perhaps they would come around once in a while and do some serious sucking up. Peeps was delighted that the BIL was absent; he always thought of him as a real lout. The real issue, of course, was that since the oldest boy disappeared, their marriage was on the rocks. Neither wanted a divorce —— they could not afford it. The Sister had gone back to work after decades out of the job market; she was bright and personable and managed to land at a small marketing company in Glenview. She made sixteen an hour with a promised bump to twenty after six months. She worked her ass off to make sure this worked out. She took great pride in having an income that was not her husband's; he mocked her for how little she made; she told him to fuck off. That is what a McAvoy would say under the circumstances.

The big news in Peeps' little world was that Dominick's had filed for bankruptcy; Terry did not know if they were filing to reorganize and get out from a mound of debt or if they planned to liquidate the company. As Terry reported all of this, he was sure that they would not find anyone to take over the stores, even at a very reduced bankruptcy price. The stores were old and dirty, they had not been remodeled for a decade. Selection was limited as many vendors refused to ship without a check. Employees were leaving in droves, which made managing his store very difficult for Terry. He spent at least half his day stocking shelves and handling customer complaints—which were highly vocal and constant. Some blamed the problem on Terry personally, as though he ran the entire chain himself. All management employees got a twenty-five percent reduction in pay immediately. One assistant quit without even telling Terry and then had the nerve to ask for a reference after the fact. Terry refused and hung up the phone.

Peeps was so relieved that they had settled with Dominick's well over a year ago and he was protected because the remaining money due him was in the form of an annuity controlled not by the company but by a highly rated insurance company. Peeps asked Terry about home life and found out that it was not very good and with the pending failure of Dominick's it would get worse; his wife had refused to find a job after the kids were in high school. Terry wondered what she did all day—something Peeps could relate to. Terry said that he had started cutting expenses months ago; the cleaning lady was gone; he cut up all but one of their charge cards and economized on food and entertainment. His wife was furious but she really could not say much; if she opened her eyes, she would know what was coming and it was not going to be pretty.

One by one, stores were closing. Only the ones with high sales remained open—Terry's store was number fourteen on the list, so it would buy him some time. He spent every minute he could on company time looking for a job; he called, faxed his resume, followed up and tried every trick in the book to get employers' attention. He spent the evenings online going through various job sites and trying to tailor his resume and cover letter to the posting. To his surprise and relief he started to get interviews, and from some surprising places. His most promising was from Chase Bank; they were forming a group internally specializing in retail financing, bankruptcy, and mergers and acquisitions. They needed someone who knew what actually went on in retail stores. The offer came through at just over five percent higher than what he had been making, including his bonus. He jumped on it and spent every free moment learning about Chase, where they made their money and what the culture was like.

When he got his formal offer letter, he resigned with two weeks' notice. Human Resources, what was left of them, told him to leave his keys in his office and anything else that belonged to the company. He went straight to Peeps' house, letter in hand, and insisted that they go to the Bubble for drinks. It was eleven o'clock in the morning, so Peeps made sure that they both had a hot dog before drinking. After a couple of martinis they were wondering why Larry and his business did not have a street named after it. They thought it was hilarious to have Double Bubble Way above the Norwood Avenue Street sign; honorary street names were used all the time to recognize local people or businesses. They agreed that one day Larry was sure to have his name on a sign. Three martinis later, they wobbled to Peeps' house and fell sound asleep in the living room where Christy found them some hours later.

Weeks went by and Terry called and invited himself for Sunday dinner. He was highly agitated when he came in and two martinis did not calm him down. He did not ask for help, just blurted out that he was sure he had made a mistake taking the Chase job. He did not know what he was doing there or what he was supposed to do or how to act. He was part of a fifteen-member team assigned to look for retail businesses in the Midwest, including online ventures and even companies that were closing down. Their perfect customer would have been Dominick's—helping them to reorganize or liquidate and take on the creditors on behalf of the owners. He was really desperate to get his shit together; he hardly knew anyone in the group, being one of the last hired. He could not go to his boss and ask what he was supposed to do. Peeps suggested doing research on companies in trouble and presenting a prospectus to the group on which companies they should approach. Christy had a better idea. Everyone knew that retail was in serious trouble; why go after failures, although the bank could make a lot of money working out their problems or finding a buyer. She suggested that he use his skills to look for internet retailers who wanted to expand or get right with the banks and creditors.

They talked for two hours about Christy's idea, meanwhile Peeps forgot about the pork roast which was now toast. After ordering pasta from a local joint, they began to look into Chicago-based companies and how they were doing and which of them might need help. In an hour, Terry had a short list of about twenty firms and a full belly. He was relieved and thankful; Peeps reminded him it was the least they could do as he had helped him over the years many times. They heard nothing from Terry for nearly three months, until he arrived unannounced one Saturday night with a bottle of very fine champagne and a huge grin on his face. Over the months he called the team together and made presentations on one ailing cosmetic chain and four online businesses, all of whom wanted to grow. The team decided that four of the five were perfect for their mission and signed them up as clients, which got everyone a bonus for their efforts. He also reported that he and the wife had pretty much patched things up, including getting the cleaning lady back. It was not nirvana, but it was the best it had been in years. The kids particularly noticed and they were a family again. Peeps and Christy casually mentioned that they were planning a modest trip to Italy, with most of the time in Rome. They were vague on details and itinerary.

In point of fact, they were well into their planning, again a late October trip to avoid crowds and the heat. For reasons he could not figure out, Peeps was particularly sensitive to heat; he sweated when he should be comfortable. He found himself putting the air conditioning on even when it was seventy degrees out. He made sure that Zava would have rooms that were cool at night, or he would die. Christy thought he ought to see Dr. Frank before going on the trip; Peeps, of course, lost and Christy won. She came to the appointment for a full physical and went away with a script for high blood pressure. The meds helped a bit, but in general he felt vaguely shitty most days. He agreed after the trip, he would go back and ask for more tests.

They loved Rome but it was not Paris; the driver was excellent and they had passes for all the important sights from the Vatican Gardens to Michelangelo in Florence. They had a great time, but Peeps tired out more quickly and they tended to go to their room earlier—about the time most Romans were just sitting down for dinner. The weather changed every day; hot then cold. Peeps could never figure out what to wear. He sweated through the day mostly. Having said this, the trip was a huge success and they vowed to find other places they wanted to go. God knows there were a million spectacular sites in Europe alone. When they got home, Peeps was having a hard time getting the luggage up the stairs. The limo driver came to his assistance and Peeps retreated to the bedroom to rest. Christy got on the phone with Dr. Frank and asked that more work be done on Peeps; there was a problem and it needed to be fixed soon. In three days, much to their amazement, Peeps found himself under a CAT scan for a full body review. The problem was fairly obvious and easily solved; Peeps had a small blood clot and medicine would take care of the problem in two or three weeks. The McAvoys returned home relieved and grateful for the quick action to find out what was wrong. Peeps was told to take it easy and not use anything, like little blue pills, that would increase blood pressure. They did not want this clot to travel.

A month or so passed, and Peeps felt better—not great but decent. He was bored and was looking for things to do. He decided to start going to the Newberry again to write short articles about the Chicago fire and its aftermath. He checked in with Gilmour and, yes, he would edit without mercy, of course. Their book was about to come out; they got an offer with an advance from Sourcebooks, a Naperville independent publisher, who took a century to get the book published but otherwise was excellent. They had advance sales of about a thousand copies, not a bestseller but not bad for a start. Gilmour had three dozen people, many prominent, review the book on Amazon. There were glowing reviews on the back cover of the book; Peeps was sure that they had never read a word but wrote their comments from a script provided by Gilmour. He guessed that every author did the same. The reviews were a game, but if they got the book higher on Amazon's sales list, well so be it.

So it was back on the bus a few days a week, this time without a real goal in mind, He talked to Gilmour about doing articles on some of the people or events out of the book. Gilmour thought that would be a great way to get publicity for the book. Peeps was realistic enough that his chances of getting a print article were slim, but he tried. He had a thousand-word sample ready to go and sent it to the *Sun Times, Tribune, Chicago Magazine* and the *Southtown*; he proposed a three or four article series. Not only did he not get any takers, but the fuckers refused to even respond. Gilmour took over in trying to place an article or two, but even he failed. Peeps went online and found blogs and other sites about Chicago and its history; most of them were political and would only consider any material that talked about corruption in Chicago. That was no problem as more than half the book was devoted to the nefarious and greedy. He had some small success, but every one of the sites butchered the length and content to fit their needs. Their big break came when Gilmour was invited to appear on WTTW television, the local public TV station. Phil Ponce interviewed Gilmour for nearly ten minutes. This was followed by a three-minute segment on WGN television at the noon hour. The guys were not sure what the publisher was doing, although Barnes & Noble reordered, which was a good sign.

The authors received their first royalty statement with a nice check enclosed. They never did find an agent; no matter, it worked out just as well. They had sold just over six thousand copies, print and electronic; most sales were online so they did not expect to be dinged by returns from booksellers. Enclosed was a very crabby note from their editor, Pamela, demanding their new book proposal. Is that how this works, they both wondered? They met at lunch to plot their strategy and decided to focus on the Chicago fire and do a series of profiles of important and not so important people affected by the fire. Once again Peeps' job was to look for the unusual, outrageous and the downright nasty people whose lives were mangled by the fire. They sent a short synopsis and made up bios of the type of profiles that would be in the book. Pamela sent a contract a week later, with a larger advance and a better royalty rate. Back to work as they smiled their way to the bank.

CHAPTER TWELVE:
Sic transit gloria mundi

There was an old tradition that when a new pope was inaugurated, one of the priests in the procession would kneel down at intervals and repeat the phrase *sic transit gloria mundi*—thus goes the glory of the world. It was a reminder to the new pope not to confuse elevation to pope and getting involved in the trappings of the world. In the end he would be dust just like everyone else. The phrase was a reminder to everyone that worldly matters do not go along forever or in the same fashion. It was a lesson in humility. Basically, shit happens.

The first round of shit was the news that their neighbor had cancer again, and it was serious. Peeps and Christy talked endlessly about what they might say or do. Peeps had known the family for years and they often came to the McAvoy house for Christmas dinner. Christy only knew them from the last ten years, during which the family was preoccupied with helping raise their grandchildren. They were private people and certainly did not want to discuss their troubles with everyone in the neighborhood. On the other hand, Peeps felt a special friendship with the family. In the end, they decided to send a card over expressing their love and concern and that if they could help in any way, please call; even if they just wanted to come over for wine and a chance to talk Christy and Peeps would be there for them. It was not much, but it was the best they could think to do. A note came back several days later thanking them and they would call if they needed anything, signed N.

Round two was much less personal, but much sadder. A young couple had moved into the Flynn house and did a masterful job of renovating both inside and out. The couple was just married and were one of the five gay couples who had moved on to Hood Street in recent years. Peeps had only met Leo twice and just in passing; they both introduced themselves and Peeps admired the changes to the house. Apparently, friends and family had not heard from the men for several days and the police were called to do a well-being check. Because they could not see in, the police forced the back door only to be hit with the smell of death. Both men were drug users and were found in the family room with drugs and paraphernalia all around them. The neighborhood rumor mill went wild with speculation that they were hardcore drug dealers. According to the experts, the house was filled with drugs, cash, and guns. Nothing of the sort was true; they were reported as occasional users and had simply consumed bad drugs. This terrible event shocked the hell out of the entire neighborhood.

Plague three began when Terry came to visit; they had not seen him for months. He was invited for Sunday dinner and accepted. Peeps was making a basic pasta and salad, so one more was no big deal. They settled down in the front room with the baseball game on low and talked over drinks. Peeps sensed almost immediately that there was something wrong, so he ventured first, assuming that it was work related. No, in fact, work could not be better; in fact, their team had expanded and Terry was one of the two group leaders. His career change had gone far better than he ever thought. During dinner Terry reported that his wife had filed for divorce and that he had prostate cancer, the very aggressive form. No sitting around and dying of old age; this would kill him in a year. Terry asked if he could move into the basement again. Peeps said it had not been cleaned for months, but he was welcome; Terry even had the basement door key from his last stay. Peeps helped him carry luggage into the house, as best he could. Terry was going in for radical surgery to remove the entire prostate, knowing the probability of incontinence and impotence. The impotence had already begun and thus the divorce. Christy discreetly excused herself so that the guys could talk.

Shitty problem four had already happened, they just did not know about it yet. A month later, they went out for dinner with Ralphy and in passing he mentioned that he would need open heart surgery; the blockage was severe. This tale was told, of course, over drinks and rare steaks. Hearing this news made Christy so upset she almost made a scene in the restaurant. His most recent ex-wife offered to move in after surgery to help him recover. Christy was relieved that someone would be there; she could not help him at all, although she was very willing. The prognosis was very good, but Ralphy would have to make major changes in his lifestyle—he could have meat, just not that much of it. Cigars were out and one drink a night was all he could expect. Physical therapy would go on for months, and as he was so out of shape, it would be a slow go at best. Some good news at last: Ralphy went to a rehab facility and was doing just fine. He reported that his therapists were nothing but sadistic bitches and he called them that regularly and often. Christy smiled—an ideal patient.

The plagues were interrupted for a few months; Christy had heard about a new kind of surgery and therapy for blind people. They drove to the University of Chicago Hospital to investigate and she was encouraged to sign up for the program. She had weekly appointments which made her asshole boss crazy; Christy had her priorities set and if she could even get some slight sight to return she would be thrilled. The day of the surgery, Peeps was so nervous that he must have gone to the bathroom six times in two hours. She would be bandaged for weeks, not that it made a difference; no matter what the doctors did they could not make matters worse. She stayed in the hospital for two days and was released to Peeps' loving care. Nothing changed, except that Christy had a ridiculous bandage over her head. He did not think she needed to know the details. In four weeks they would know if there was any change; the doctors warned her not to have great expectations. This was on the cutting edge of eye surgery.

The four weeks dragged on like prison time. Christy could not go back to work so they sat around; she knew she looked ridiculous in her bandages and was not inclined to go far. Peeps escaped by going to the Bubble regularly which did piss Christy off just a bit; he could get out, she could not. On the way home, Peeps bought a nice assortment of chocolates from Lickety Split, the sweet shop on Broadway, and took them to his neighbors. The present was received warmly by Greg but Peeps did not make any effort to go inside. He did not ask for an update and none was offered. Peeps also started going to the library again two days a week. It was a warm summer, or so it seemed to Peeps; by the time he got to the Newberry he was sweating like a pig. He had to go to the men's room to clean up before he got down to work. He talked to the new head librarian and introduced himself as co-author of a book about Chicago history. She told him that they bought three copies and had them bound as hardcover books. She thought the book very good and promised to keep an eye out for some good old-fashioned dirt during the fire era.

Peeps wisely decided to include Christy into this new project. He read outlines and synopses and asked her opinions. Christy had an old-fashioned braille machine and as Peeps dictated his content she typed it out in braille. This allowed her to really read and understand in detail and she could type out comments and suggestions. It worked out to be a very nice team effort. Their working together was noticed by Gilmour who told Peeps that the material was the best ever—the only problem was that it was going slowly. Virtually every afternoon, before cocktails and dinner, Peeps took a nap and slept like a dead man. Christy was concerned and called Dr. Frank once again. He was out of town with his family and so nothing happened for nearly a month. This made Christy very nervous.

Finally, it was time to go back to the University of Chicago Hospital to take bandages off and see what was what. Neither of them could sleep the night before and were at the hospital a full hour before their appointment. Nervous did not even come close to their feelings. They were terrified and hopeful at the same time. Peeps had the sweats and kept going to the bathroom to wash his face. When they were finally called in, they waited another twenty minutes before their research team all filed in. The protocol would call for Christy to be at the hospital two times a week for electrical stimulation of the optic nerves. They explained that this was a long-term therapy, if it was going to work at all. When they unwrapped the bandages Christy let out a yelp; she could see light and some color! There were shouts of delight and high fives all around. It was not sight but it was a start. She next got the stimulation of the optic nerves, which were surprisingly painful. She had to wear blindfolds for most of the day and was not to look directly into bright lights. She could have an hour or so a day without protection, but she was cautioned in the strictest terms to follow instructions without deviation. Next week she went back to work and she took off the blindfold in the evening when the light was low. But in her excitement she had not forgotten about Peeps.

Plague five hit them like a ton of bricks; Gilmour had not scheduled their usual monthly meeting and in fact Peeps had heard nothing from him for weeks. He tried the phone, text messages and e-mails. Finally, his son walked over to tell them what was going on. Gilmour was terminated from the firm, basically he lost his partnership; he expected that he would have to leave the firm sooner than later, but the tactless way they did it, caused Gilmour to go into deep depression and he went on a three-day bender, never leaving his apartment. The son found him passed out, wildly drunk. After a trip to the hospital, he went to a treatment center dealing with depression and alcoholism. Everyone knew that once he completed the treatment, he would return to life as usual. He was not an alcoholic, but he was depressed and used booze to take the edge off of life.

Round six was an appointment for Peeps to have an MRI. He resisted like crazy; he could not and would not sit in a long tube wrapped around him for two hours. The toughest part, beside the claustrophobia, was sitting there without moving. Christy made the appointment and made sure he was ready; the technician would give him Valium and he would be fine. She lied like a rug and everyone knew it. It was the worst day of his life, well almost. Once he got home, he went to bed for hours; he was exhausted from the anxiety and the physical ordeal of being in a tube for two hours. He literally cried himself to sleep he was so upset. Christy just stayed away and made no plans for dinner or for the evening until he came to. They had a drink and ordered a pizza which virtually went untouched. Christy was positive the light was brighter when she took off her shades. She was really excited, but kept it to herself. Ten days later, the MRI proved negative; they still could not figure out what was happening to Peeps.

After driving Christy to work, Peeps went home to shower, grab his Chromebook and backpack and head to the library. It was hot and he brought along a towel to take the sweat off his face as he walked to the bus stop. Naturally, the Broadway bus was nowhere in sight; he sat on the chairs in front of the library and fell asleep, or so he thought. At some point, he felt someone rifling through his things, taking, he thought, his phone, watch, Chromebook, his money clip and wallet. He seemed unable to do anything about it; he could not talk or move. It was as though he was frozen in place. He had the sense that people were looking at him, but he could not remain conscious. He was freezing on the hottest day of the year. At one point someone tried shaking him, calling him by name. The bus driver, who knew Peeps for years, called his supervisor and 911 at the same time. By the time the paramedics arrived, Peeps was dead.

It took the police the better part of the day to identify him; the only thing the driver could tell them was that he went by the name of Peeps. They canvassed houses on Glenlake and Norwood, but most people were at work. Toward the end of the shift, two coppers went into the Bubble for a dog and a beer. They were talking about their frustration and inability to identify this older man who had died on Broadway waiting for the bus. He had been picked clean, including his keys. The bartender overheard the name Peeps and immediately identified him. The cops felt like fools; they should have checked the bars and stores first. They found his house, but of course no one was home. Dick and Nancy had Christy's phone number and gave it to the police. They had to tell her about Peeps on the phone and promised to send a car to bring her home.

Dick and Nancy were at her house when she got home. The police called the paramedics to sedate Christy; she literally was in shock. She could not even cry; Nancy just held her while she rocked from side to side for the next hour. Then she cried tears of grief so profound that everyone in the house joined in. Nancy asked if she wanted her to call Maloney Funeral Home on Devon and Glenwood. Maloney said he would take care of everything; he just needed a signature. They managed that electronically, as Maloney lived in Northbrook, a good hour away. Christy and Dick would meet him next day late morning to finalize arrangements. Nancy took Christy's phone and began systematically to call everyone on the phone list to tell what had happened to Peeps. Everyone wanted more information, but Nancy put them off; she simply did not know what had happened. She finally got The Sister, whose name was also Nancy, and told her about her brother. By the time she was finished, there were a dozen people milling about in the front yard, not paying any attention to Peeps' garden. He would have been royally pissed if he saw what was going on in his yard.

The Sister Nancy, Christy and Dick went to the funeral parlor and were finished in an hour. Peeps had wanted a small wake before the mass of Christian burial at St. Gertrude. He was to be cremated and had left instructions for a bagpiper to play the appropriate Celtic dirges during the mass. Friends and family would be invited to Calo for lunch after. His will was up to date and of course everything went to Christy except for ten thousand to a certain Fr. Terry in Nairobi. On Saturday there was not a dry eye in the church. The bagpipe made sure of that. Terry was asked to speak a few words and he did so eloquently, without benefit of notes. This was plague seven and everyone agreed enough was enough.

Sister Nancy and Christy stood in the church before the urn, holding hands and praying. It hit Christy that she was now no longer married. Everyone had started to leave the church. Neither could cry anymore; their thoughts were about brother and husband. He was simply a fine man who spent his entire life looking for love and a future with a woman. He was a momma's boy that was for sure. He was a big, soft puppy who acted tough, but would do anything for anyone. He was complicated, but in a simple way. He was a produce clerk who co-wrote a book on Chicago. He had an alcoholic father and a loving mother whose death sent him into depression and therapy. He had become a Catholic again, with a nudge or two from Christy; nevertheless he took pride in his religion and particularly his Irish heritage. He loved the Jesuits, fascinated by the ones he came across in high school and college. He was generous to the church and the Jesuits, and would have given more if he had lived. The two went hand in glove. He could get moody, downright nasty sometimes. He loved to read history and the current pot boilers on his Kindle—he had three of them, actually. He was devoted to Christy; he never thought to stray with other women. Because he married so late, there were never any children. He thought that was alright. He had a dozen good friends and dozens more that he knew from school or the Bubble. Of course, he drank too much, but never fell down nor missed a day at work. After being hurt, he almost never complained about the pain and his loss of freedom to grow gracefully into old age. He was just a man; his parents had given the Jesuits a boy and they indeed returned a man.

EPILOGUE

Christy lasted about three months in the Hood St. house without Peeps, and called Daniel Otto to sell the house. She had decided to buy a condo in her brother's building. She hired a woman to come in each day for three hours, make dinner, clean, do the laundry, go shopping and run other necessary errands. Before she left, she would set out cereal and dishes for breakfast. Most days she had lunch with her brother, but still made time to see Nancy and other friends from the old neighborhood.

She spoke with Gilmour, who had recovered nicely, about doing Peeps' part of the book; she was fairly efficient on her computer for the blind, but would at times make horrible mistakes if she lost her way on the keyboard. Her computer had voice recognition features which made her writing and document preparation all that much easier. Getting and finding sources in braille or spoken was a problem. The librarians helped her out when they could; they also found a graduate student who was partially blind and was thrilled to be part of the project and even get paid nicely for her efforts. Christy even found that she could take the Broadway Bus, route 36, to the Newberry. Once a month she met with Gilmour at the Club to discuss progress and strategies. It just felt right.

She quit her job and signed up for Cobra for health insurance for the next eighteen months; after that, she would find coverage in the open market, but for a fortune each month. She did not care; Peeps had left her more money than she could spend. She sold every stick of furniture from Hood St. and donated the money to St. Gertrude. She went to mass at the old parish when she could talk Ralphy into driving her, which was fairly often. She saw Terry as often as possible, inviting him for holiday dinners if he had no other plans. He and his wife were divorced for the second time but Terry's health was just fine.

Otto got an obscene amount of money for the house. She was amazed. Her last day in the house, she sprinkled Peeps' ashes in the garden as he asked.

She desperately missed her mama's boy, her dear Peeps.